'Don't think too highly of me. My faults are legion,' he said, at his most sardonic.

As she put her cup aside, he rose to his feet and, taking her hands, drew her up to stand in front of him.

'If I were a better man I shouldn't be doing this,' he said, looking down at her.

The desire she saw in Charles's face was real and a little frightening in its intensity.

She held her breath as he placed her hands against his chest and put his arms round her.

The lines from *Sea Fever* on p 18 are reprinted
with the kind permission of The Society of
Authors as the literary representative of the
Estate of John Masefield

SEA
FEVER

BY

ANNE WEALE

MILLS & BOON LIMITED
ETON HOUSE   18-24 PARADISE ROAD
RICHMOND   SURREY   TW9 1SR

First published in Great Britain 1990
by Mills & Boon Limited

© Anne Weale 1990

Australian copyright 1990
Philippine copyright 1990
This edition 1990

ISBN 0 263 76685 3

Set in Times Roman 11 on 12 pt.
01-9005-49851 C

Made and printed in Great Britain

CHAPTER ONE

THE girl beached the inflatable dinghy, then straightened and stood for some moments, barefoot on the pale sand, looking back at the moonlit sloop at anchor in the deep water beyond the sharp, dangerous corals.

Sea Fever. Her home for as long as she could remember.

A riding light hung from the fore-stay, but no lights showed between decks.

From the house at the back of the beach came a burst of laughter: the baritone laughter of men and the higher-pitched sounds made by women. The girl turned and, with a resolute bracing of her shoulders, crossed the wide beach towards the garden surrounding the house.

It was the only habitation on this stretch of the coast of Bali. There was a small fishing village on the other side of the headland, but here, in this bay, only this one large house surrounded by well-kept grounds at which she had looked through binoculars before deciding to row ashore and ask for help.

Where the garden met the beach there was a wall with steps leading up to an opening in a coral stone balustrade. Inside this entrance, on both sides, were small shallow pools of water. The girl understood their purpose. Once or twice, out of curiosity, she had wandered through the grounds and public rooms of large hotels where rich Europeans and

Australians spent winter holidays. She had seen notices requesting the hotels' patrons to rinse the sand from their feet as they left the beach rather than in their bathrooms.

There was no such notice here, but she paddled in one of the pools to remove the powdering of coral from her straight toes and thin brown ankles. Had she been wearing a piece of batik-patterned cotton wrapped round her narrow hips, as she often did, she could have stood on one foot to dry the other on the hem of her sarong.

But tonight she had put on jeans and a clean shirt—her best clothes. She had once had a dress. There was a photograph of her wearing it on board *Sea Fever*, a snap taken with her parents when she was five. She couldn't remember them or the dress. While she was growing up she had always worn shorts or sarongs, with jeans on the rare occasions when something more formal was called for.

Tall palms towered over the flowering shrubs planted on the lawns of coarse springy grass on either side of the path leading up to the house. Wanting to see the people on the terrace before they saw her, she avoided the path and approached silently on the grass, keeping to the patches of dense shadow cast by the shrubs.

There were five of them: two middle-aged men and three dressed-up women. They all had drinks in their hands and, beyond them, inside the house, beneath the swirling blades of two ceiling fans, was a table laid for a dinner party. The girl had seen dinner parties taking place on the decks of large, luxurious yachts.

The first person to notice her was one of the women, who said in a startled American voice, 'Oh...where did you spring from?'

The girl advanced to the edge of the terrace. 'Good evening. I'm sorry to disturb you, but I need some advice...some help.' She looked at the older of the two men. 'Is this your house?'

Before he could reply, a sixth person appeared, a very tall, deeply tanned man who, at the sight of her, raised an enquiring eyebrow.

'Who are you?' His accent was English.

'I'm Angel...' she corrected herself, 'Evangeline Dorset. I've come from the sloop *Sea Fever*. We put in here late last night—you may have noticed us this morning. I wanted to come for help then, but Ludo wouldn't let me. He didn't believe in doctors and hospitals. He said there was nothing they could do for him. He...he died about an hour ago. He wants...wanted to be buried at sea, but I can't manage that by myself, and also I think I may need permission from the Consul or someone.'

It was only by an effort of will that she managed to keep her voice steady and unemotional. She couldn't show her true feelings in front of these strangers to whom her intrusion upon a festive occasion must come as a nuisance.

'Who was Ludo? Your father?' asked a red-haired woman, the most glamorous of the three.

'My grandfather.'

'Were you alone with him? Is there no one else on board with you?' This question came from the man she had spoken to first.

Angel shook her head. 'Just the two of us.'

'Good lord . . . poor child!' he said, looking concerned. 'What a distressing situation!'

His sympathetic tone made her throat tighten, her eyes prickle with tears. She was glad when the tall man said briskly, 'You'd better come to my office and I'll find out what has to be done.'

As she followed him past the table laid for dinner and across the large room to another leading off it, she heard the woman with red hair say, 'What a bore! I hope Charles can sort it out quickly. One feels sorry for her, of course, but it is a bit much...'

She left the remark unfinished and perhaps the man called Charles, now several strides ahead of Angel, hadn't heard it. Was she his wife? she wondered.

By the time she reached his office he had switched on a desk light and another overhead fan. He sat down behind the large desk, indicating with one hand that she should sit down in front of the desk and picking up a pen with the other.

'Was your grandfather's surname the same as yours?'

'Yes . . . Ludovic Dorset.'

She watched him jot it down, the nib of the gold-banded tortoiseshell pen moving swiftly over the notepad, leaving a line of flowing black writing.

His hands, like his face, were very brown and not, she noticed, those of what Ludo would have called a desk-wallah. Whatever this man did in his office—there was a computer screen and keyboard on a smaller desk and other pieces of equipment she didn't recognise—he didn't look like a sedentary person. His shoulders were in proportion to his height and his body was lean and muscular, as

powerful as Ludo's had been when she was small
and he had swung her up to ride on his shoulders.
He had been seventy then, but still a formidable
man. It was only in the past year that he had
become old and frail.

'And the boat...*Sea Fever*, yes? Where's she
registered?'

'She's out of Brixham in Devon, but that was a
long time ago...before I was born. I've never been
to England.'

'But that's where your family come from...where
your other relations are?'

He looked up from the pad and gave her a
searching stare with his curiously cold grey eyes.
She was used to Ludo's kind blue eyes which had
looked at the world with good-humoured tolerance. Those were not the characteristics suggested
by the handsome face on the other side of the desk.
She recognised his good looks but couldn't define
the qualities she saw in his face. She knew only that
he was a type of man she had never encountered
before and wasn't certain she liked.

'I have no other relations...or none that I know
of.'

'I see. How old are you, Angel?'

He missed nothing, she thought, remembering
how swiftly she had substituted her rather old-
fashioned first name for the pet name first used by
her parents and then by her grandfather. She had
been named after his wife who, like her namesake,
had never been called by her full name but always
Eva.

'I'm eighteen...almost.'

Again his right eyebrow shot up, this time in patent scepticism. 'Are you sure? You don't look more than fifteen.'

'Quite sure,' she answered firmly. 'I have a birth certificate to prove it. I'll be eighteen in March.'

The chair in which she was sitting was far enough from the desk for him to be able to flash an appraising glance from her neck to her blue-jeaned knees, taking in the boyishly slim lines of the body between those points.

No doubt it was her extreme slenderness which made him say, 'When did you last eat?'

She couldn't remember. Normally she had a good appetite, but the past twenty-four hours had been too fraught for her to think about food.

'I—I don't know, but I'm not hungry.'

'Do you know the cause of your grandfather's death? You're certain he *is* dead? Not comatose?'

'I'm certain. His heart gave out. He'd been taking pills for a heart condition, but they weren't working any more. He felt poorly all yesterday and this morning, he didn't get up. He just lay in his bunk, talking sometimes...but very weak. He knew he was dying. He...he even said goodbye.'

In spite of her resolve not to show the anguish she felt, her eyes filled with tears. She tried to blink them back, but two overflowed and began to trickle down her cheeks.

'I'm sorry,' she muttered huskily, striving to recover control, wiping the tears away with her fingertips.

At this moment a Balinese man in a dark brown silk tunic worn with a sarong appeared in the doorway.

Speaking the lingua franca of Indonesia, the man behind the desk said to him, 'Bring a light supper on a tray, please. The meal for my guests may proceed without me. This young woman is in trouble. Her grandfather has died on the boat which came yesterday.'

While he was speaking, he produced a folded, unused handkerchief which he handed across the desk to Angel.

As his servant bowed and disappeared, he took the receiver from the telephone and dialled a number. As he waited for it to answer, he looked, not at her, but at a large Balinese painting on the wall.

A few moments later, he said, 'Charles Thetford here. Sorry to trouble you out of office hours, but I thought you were the best person to advise me on the proper procedure when a yachtsman dies on board his boat. Natural causes, and he expressed a wish to be buried at sea.'

Angel could hear the voice at the other end of the line, but not clearly enough to follow what was being said. She wiped her eyes and blew her nose, reluctant to use the fine white linen handkerchief but having no option as, foolishly, she had failed to bring one with her.

Presently Charles Thetford put his hand over the mouthpiece and asked, 'Was your grandfather a religious man? Would he wish for a priest or a clergyman to officiate at his burial?'

She shook her head. 'He had his own religion. He asked me to read his favourite poem over him. That was all he wanted.'

She expected to see his eyebrow lift disapprovingly, but he only nodded and told the man on the line that none of the conventional funeral rites would be required.

He was still on the telephone when the manservant came back, carrying a tray on which was a covered dish, a tall glass of fruit juice, a small basket of bread and a pot of butter.

At his employer's signal, he placed the tray on Angel's side of the desk before indicating that, if she stood up, he would move the chair forward for her. When she was seated again, he whipped the cover off the dish, revealing a lightly cooked omelette.

The sight of it made Angel realise that it was twenty-four hours since last she had eaten. Today she had had nothing but coffee to keep her going. She still wasn't hungry but, presented with the omelette, she knew that she ought to eat something. She stretched out her hand for the glass and, lifting it to her lips, sipped. It was the most delicious juice she had ever tasted, ice-cold and wonderfully refreshing.

Something had gone wrong with the refrigerator on *Sea Fever* while they were island-hopping in the Flores Sea to the east of Bali. Ludo hadn't been able to repair the fault and it was several weeks since they had enjoyed cold drinks. The chilled juice was so good the sip became a long swallow, followed by another. She could easily have drained the glass, but forced herself to replace it on the tray, half full.

Conscious that Mr Thetford was no longer looking at the painting but now had his eyes on her, she unfolded the starched cotton napkin, folded like the petals of a lotus flower on the side plate, and spread it across her lap in the way Ludo had taught her.

He had not always been a sea-gypsy, roving from island to island across the Pacific Ocean and then up through the seas surrounding the vast archipelago of Indonesian islands as far north as the Gulf of Siam. Until the death of his wife he had been a weekend sailor, spending the rest of his time in London, one of the leading barristers of his day. But there must always have been a streak of rootlessness in him, for at fifty, desolated by the death of his adored Eva, he had thrown his career aside for a life of travel and adventure.

Unfortunately, thirty years of inflation, and some unsuccessful speculations, had steadily reduced his financial resources. In recent years he had been hard pressed to make ends meet.

'When I go you'll have to sell her and find yourself a shore berth, my darling,' he had told Angel, many times.

Now he had gone, leaving her completely alone in the world, with only the tiny income—nothing like enough to live on—from his remaining investments, and the sloop, long overdue for refit and not likely to fetch much of a price since she wasn't the type of vessel to appeal to people with money. They went in for wide-beamed motor yachts with powerful turbo-diesel engines and opulent fittings. Even sailing vessels were required to have aluminium masts, self-furling sails, electric winches and air-conditioning between decks.

Sea Fever needed skill and muscle-power to sail her. She had an auxiliary engine but was built to be driven by the four winds of heaven. The thought of parting with the sloop, the only home she had ever had or wanted to have, sent a thrust of panic through Angel. Her hand shook as she picked up the fork and forced herself to cut off a corner of the omelette.

She was woken out of a deep sleep by someone shaking her shoulder and opened her eyes to find a Balinese woman bending over her.

'You get up now... have bath... put clothes on. I put water in bath. You get up, please.'

With no clear idea where she was, still more than half asleep, Angel let herself be led to a bathroom where the woman helped her to undress and then bundled her long sun-streaked hair inside a plastic shower cap.

'I come back in five minutes... bring clean clothes. Tuan Thetford not like being kept waiting,' she informed Angel gravely.

At first, submerging herself in the lukewarm scented water, Angel still felt confused and disorientated. Then she began to remember the events of the previous evening, but with no recollection of how she had come to spend the night in Charles Thetford's house instead of returning to the sloop.

The last thing she remembered was the small, soft-footed manservant removing the first tray and bringing another with coffee on it while the owner of the house made some more telephone calls.

Could she have fallen asleep in his office? It wasn't impossible. She had been awake, worrying, most of the previous night, and yesterday, knowing that Ludo was leaving her, had been the worst day of her life.

Tears filled her eyes as she thought of him holding her hand in a clasp which had suddenly become pitiably feeble compared with his former strong grip.

'I shouldn't have let it come to this,' he had murmured. 'I should have let you go long ago. But I couldn't bear to part with you. You're so like her...so like my Eva. I've been a selfish old man...it was wrong of me to keep you with me. You should have been training for a career. Women need to stand on their own feet...not to rely on a man. It's all changed since I was young.'

And then he had started to ramble about the world in his youth and the girl he had fallen in love with, the most beautiful débutante of 1937, Evangeline Chesterfield, whose suitors had included two aristocrats but who had turned them all down to marry him.

The Balinese woman came back and saw Angel lying in the bath with tears streaming down her face.

She bent over her and gently stroked Angel's hair, saying in the language common to all the islands of Indonesia, 'Yes, weep, but weep for yourself, not for the venerable man whose spirit has gone elsewhere. Death is a joyful release for those who have lived good lives.'

She straightened and used a corner of the towel folded over her arm to dry the girl's cheeks before opening it out and holding it ready to enfold Angel when she stood up.

* * *

An hour later, wearing white, the colour of mourning in Bali, Angel stood on the deck of *Sea Fever* as the sloop headed into the dawn of a new day.

Her sails were furled and she was propelled by her engine, with a Balinese man at the helm. There were a number of men on board: the doctor who had signed Ludovic Dorset's death certificate, the official who had given permission for him to be buried at sea and two strong young fishermen from the nearby village who knew a place where the sea was many fathoms deep and would lower him over the side there.

While Angel was sleeping, the rites of death had been performed by others, and now her grandfather's long form, shrouded in stout cloth and weighted, lay on the deck, strewn with flowers.

Beside her stood the Balinese maid, whose name was Lila, with a silk sash round her waist, the sash all Balinese wore when they entered a temple or followed a funeral procession on the way to the colourful public cremations which were an essential part of their culture.

Angel guessed that Charles Thetford had asked Lila to come with them in case she broke down. But she felt calm and composed now, and deeply grateful to him for making himself responsible for all the arrangements needed to carry out her grandfather's wishes. In spite of a certain hardness about the set of his mouth, he must be a kind-hearted man.

He had even remembered the poem which was to be Ludo's valediction, and asked if she needed to read it and, if so, where the book containing it was to be found.

'I know it by heart,' she had told him. 'It's John Masefield's *Sea Fever*. Ludo learnt it at school and I learned it from him when I was a little girl.'

They were several miles off the coast of Bali when they came to the place where his body would be given to the ocean. The helmsmen cut the motor and the sloop glided over the calm surface of the sea, now tinged with red as the sun rose above the horizon.

Angel, who had been facing the bows with her back to the others, now turned towards the stern. She looked at Charles Thetford. With his dark hair ruffled by the breeze, he looked rather less intimidating than her initial impression of him. He gave a slight nod of the head, at the same time unfolding his arms which had been crossed over his chest and clasping his hands behind him in a more formal posture. Whereas some tall men she had seen were inclined to stoop or to slouch, Mr Thetford was like her grandfather, whose bearing, even in his eighties, had always been upright, giving him—as it did the younger man—an air of innate authority.

She looked down at the old man's remains and wondered if his long life had really come to an end or if, as Buddhists believed, his spirit was setting out on a new stage of the long path to enlightenment.

Lifting her chin and raising her eyes to the sky— now ablaze with fiery streaks—she began to recite the poem she had learned at Ludo's knee.

' ' 'I must down to the seas again, to the lonely sea and the sky, And all I ask is a tall ship and a star to steer her by...' ' '

As the great glowing orb of the sun cleared the line of the horizon, the dark outline of Bali became bathed in golden light. Memories of all the land-falls they had made together flitted through Angel's mind as she came to the poem's last lines.

' ' '...And all I ask is a merry yarn from a laughing fellow-rover, And quiet sleep and a sweet dream when the long trick's over.' ' '

At a signal from Charles Thetford, the fisher-men stepped forward, raised the board on which the shrouded form lay and carried it to the rails. Angel looked up at the sky again and remembered a line from another of John Masefield's poems— *'Death opens unknown doors'*.

A few moments later there was a splash and it was over. When she went to the side and looked down, all that remained were the flowers, floating on the sunlit sea.

'I don't know how to thank you for your kindness, Mr Thetford,' she said, looking up at him as the sloop returned to her anchorage near the beach in front of his house. She was tall herself, but her head barely reached his shoulder.

'I was glad to be of service,' he said courteously.

Sea Fever's dinghy was still on the beach where Angel had left it. She and the rest of the funeral party had come aboard in a power launch used by Charles Thetford and his guests for water-skiing.

Angel would have liked to say goodbye and watch them go ashore while she stayed on the sloop and began to come to terms with being on her own. However, because she had to recover her clothes—the white blouse and skirt she was wearing had been loaned by one of the three women she had seen on the terrace last night—and also the sloop's tender, she was obliged to go ashore with them. Later in the day she would have to make one brief final trip ashore to return Mr Thetford's washed and ironed handkerchief to him.

There was no sign of any of his guests when they returned to the house. Much to Angel's relief, both the doctor and the Consular official declined an invitation to stay for breakfast. Their deferential manner towards him seemed to confirm her intuitive feeling that he was someone of great power and influence. Yet he was many years younger than the two men staying with him.

'I must change back into my own clothes,' she said, when the doctor and the Consul had gone.

'They won't be ready for you yet. The sun hasn't been up long enough to dry this morning's laundry,' said her host. 'We'll have breakfast in the gazebo where our conversation won't disturb my late-rising friends. I've told them they're missing the best hour of the day but have failed to persuade them to change their habits.'

The gazebo was a kind of summer-house built at one end of the long balustraded wall between his grounds and the beach. It had a roof supported by four corner pillars. Its low walls were a continuation of the balustrade with a bench built round three sides and a table in the middle. The bench had been made comfortable for them with indigo and white batik squabs and cushions and the table was being laid by the manservant, who this morning was wearing a starched cotton tunic with his sarong which was tied in the Balinese way with a fish-tail effect at the front.

He had five or six other servants under his command, and they came back and forth from wherever the food was prepared to the gazebo at the unhurried pace of people bred in a climate where, within an hour of sunrise, the temperature began to soar and metal left in the sun soon became too hot to handle.

'Do you like tea or coffee for breakfast?' Charles Thetford enquired.

'Tea, please.' The question reminded Angel of the coffee she had drunk last night before falling asleep where she sat.

'I'm sorry about last night...going to sleep in your office, I mean. I can't understand why I didn't wake up when they hauled me off to bed.' She assumed that two of the servants must have carried her to the room where she'd slept.

'You didn't wake up because you were sedated. There was a herb in your coffee which helps people to black out for a few hours when that's what they need. I use it myself occasionally. It's not like a chemical sleeping pill and has none of their side effects.'

'You mean you *drugged* me?' she exclaimed.

It was her first intimation that he was not only rich and influential but ruthless as well. Perhaps it was only men with a ruthless streak who achieved power at his age, or indeed any age.

CHAPTER TWO

'I THOUGHT you needed a rest. I made sure you had one,' Charles Thetford answered calmly.

Angel nibbled her full lower lip, a habit of hers when in doubt. It seemed impolite to reprove someone who had been so helpful. At the same time she felt she must say what she thought of his arbitrary action.

'I realise your intention was kind, but I don't think you should have done that without my knowledge. Ludo says... Ludo used to say that good ends never justify bad means.'

'In general your grandfather was right, but there are exceptions to every rule. Will you have some of this rice?'

He had removed the cover from a dish of lightly fried rice mixed with bits of chicken and vegetables.

Angel found she was hungry. 'Yes, please.' She helped herself.

As she handed the serving spoon to him their fingertips brushed and she felt a curious sensation quite different from any ordinary casual physical contact. It would have been an exaggeration to describe it as like touching a live wire, and indeed she had never had that experience. But it was the comparison which came into her mind. The sensation startled and puzzled her. As she waited for him to finish serving himself before she began to eat, she wondered if it could have been an after-effect of the herb he had given her. The drug, whatever it was, might have no side effects on him but perhaps could produce some strange reactions in other people. This was the only explanation she could think of for the very odd feeling, like a charge of electric power, which had shot up her arm as the spoon changed hands.

They ate in silence for some minutes until he said, 'Tell me something about yourself, Angel.'

'There's not much to tell. Both my parents were killed in an accident when I was five, so Ludo took charge of me. I've lived with him ever since.'

'On board *Sea Fever*?'

'Yes.'

'What about schooling?'

'When I was twelve Ludo thought about sending me away to boarding school. But it would have been very expensive...the fees and flying back and forth to wherever he was for the holidays. He'd been teaching me himself up to then and he felt that I knew as much as most girls of my age, so he decided to go on giving me lessons. He didn't think much of the curricula at schools he made enquiries about. He felt they were all geared to passing exams, not to the development of girls' individual talents.'

'What are your particular talents?'

'I don't think I have any. I can't draw and although I like music I've never wanted to learn to play an instrument. My abilities are mostly practical. I can do all the things one needs to live on a boat.'

'Can you navigate?'

'Of course. I could do that by the time I was eight. It's rather essential knowledge if there are only two of you on board. If Ludo had ever been taken ill at sea, or had some sort of accident, I should have had to take over as skipper.'

'My knowledge of sailing is confined to much smaller boats than your grandfather's sloop. But I should have thought *Sea Fever* needed at least two people to sail her.'

'Ideally, yes. Before I was old enough to be useful, Ludo generally had someone to crew for him, although he did sail her single-handed at times. I shall have to find someone to crew for me. Is there a bus service along this road?' she asked.

'Yes, two or three buses a day, I believe. Why do you ask?'

'Tomorrow I might go to Kuta and see if I can find an Aussie who knows how to sail and fancies a few months at sea. Once or twice, when our funds were a bit low, we did some chartering, and that's how I'll have to earn my living from now on. There are always back-packers stopping off in Kuta on their way to Europe or India. I'll go to Made's *warung*. They might let me put up a notice advertising for a crew.'

It occurred to her that he might not know about Made's, an open-fronted eating place on one of the main streets in Kuta, where she and Ludo had often had a meal and watched the world go by. But it wasn't the sort of place that rich people patronised.

'Made's is where young people, hard-up people, eat,' she explained.

'I know Made's . . . and the clientele includes a sprinkling of people I wouldn't trust further than I could throw them,' he added drily.

'You can say that about any cheap eating place, and probably about expensive restaurants too.' Angel drank from a glass of the same mixture of fruit juices she had had the night before. 'I'm quite a good judge of character. Ludo taught me. He was a lawyer when he was young and he knew a lot about dishonest people.'

Charles Thetford finished his rice. 'Your plan isn't practical,' he told her. 'A girl of your age can't charter for a living. Even if you were older...in your middle twenties...it would be a dodgy undertaking. At seventeen it would be folly.'

'Almost eighteen...and I haven't any choice. It's the only thing I can do.'

'I realise that you don't want to sell a boat which has been your home since you were a little girl, but I'm afraid that's what you'll have to do,' he said firmly. 'It looks to me as if the sloop could do with a refit, so you won't get a very good price for her, but you should make enough to tide you over until you can earn your living in a more suitable way.'

'I wouldn't dream of selling *Sea Fever*,' she said, shocked at the suggestion. 'I'd be like a crab without its shell. Where would I live? Where would I go?'

She had been speaking rhetorically, but he answered as if she had been asking his advice.

'Why not try England first? It's where your grandfather practised law, I presume? You're British by birth, aren't you?'

'Yes, I was born in London, but I've never wanted to go back there. The only cities which appeal to me are Paris and Venice and New York.'

'You wouldn't be allowed to work in America without a permit, and in France and Italy you'd have a language problem. England would be the easiest place for you to make a start.'

Angel shook her head. 'I don't want to go to England. I prefer it here...not necessarily here in Bali but in this part of the world. I'd like to visit Europe one of these days, but I'd rather live somewhere in south-east Asia or the Pacific. I feel this is where I belong.'

He was about to reply when his attention was distracted. He rose to his foot. 'Good morning.'

Turning to look over her shoulder, Angel saw the woman with red hair strolling towards them. She was wearing a brilliantly-coloured kimono and didn't appear to have anything on underneath it. Her breasts, which were moving slightly as she walked, were clearly outlined by the thin silk.

'Good morning, darling.' As she entered the gazebo she lifted her cheek for a kiss and Charles stooped to brush it lightly with his lips.

'Come and sit between us,' he said, standing aside for her to seat herself facing the sea. 'I don't think you two have been properly introduced,' he added. 'This is Leonora York, Angel.'

'How do you do,' said Angel. So she wasn't his wife, or not yet. Perhaps they were engaged. 'Is it you I have to thank for lending me these clothes for the funeral?'

'No, they belong to Amy. I'm so sorry about your grandfather.'

If she hadn't overheard the remark Leonora had made the night before, Angel would have thought her sympathy was genuine. As it was, she couldn't help wondering if Charles had also overheard and had remonstrated with his fiancée or girlfriend, which was why she was being nicer this morning.

'Thank you. Of course I shall miss him dreadfully, but he was eighty-two and he wasn't ill for very long. He would have loathed ending his days as an invalid,' she said, striving to sound if not cheerful at least philosophical. She knew that her grief could only be an embarrassment to these people who didn't know her and had never met Ludo.

'We've just been discussing Angel's future,' said Charles. 'She will probably take your advice more seriously than mine, Leonora. Wouldn't you agree with my view that her plan to employ someone to crew for her and try to make a living chartering is out of the question?'

'I really wouldn't know,' said Leonora. 'My knowledge of the yachting world wouldn't cover the head of a pin.'

'But you know what it's like to be a girl of seventeen...going on eighteen,' he amended, catching Angel's eye, a hint of amusement in his own. 'Would you have wanted to be alone at sea with some guy you'd picked up in Kuta on the strength of his claim to be a competent crew?'

'I wouldn't have wanted to be alone at sea with anyone,' said Leonora. 'Yachting isn't my idea of fun, except possibly on something the size of Khashoggi's floating palace. I shouldn't mind a cruise on that. Talking of Kuta, I'd like to go back to the shop where I bought my batik skirt and get them to take in the waist a couple of inches. Could we do that today?'

'Why don't you and Amy and Maureen go together? You don't need me to help you shop.'

'I hate shopping with other women. I'd rather go on my own... but it would be more fun with you.'

Ignoring the rider, Charles said, 'In that case take the car and go by yourself. Last night the others were planning to spend today relaxing and I shall be busy most of the day.'

'You're supposed to be relaxing as well,' she reminded him, laying a beautifully manicured hand on his muscular forearm.

'I am relaxing. Merely being here relaxes me.' His gaze swept from the projecting headland to the point where the island's coastline curved away out of sight. Then his eyes came back to the anchored sloop. 'When was *Sea Fever* built?' he asked Angel.

Reluctant to admit how old the sloop was, she said, 'She was built just before World War II for a man who went into the Navy and was killed in action. So she was laid up for years and was virtually new when Ludo bought her in 1958. Not long ago we read about a six-berth cruising yacht, built in 1930, selling for three-quarters of a million dollars. She was much larger than *Sea Fever*, with a fireplace in the saloon, but it does show that age isn't necessarily a disadvantage if the boat was well built in the first place.'

'But nowadays cedar hulls, teak decks and mahogany fittings have to be combined with the latest developments in marine electronics and hydraulics to fetch the sort of price you've mentioned,' said Charles. 'The latest thing is satellite navigation. I have an interest in a British company making that equipment. It can fix a yacht's position to within a couple of metres, I'm told.'

'Yes, and it can break down. All that new stuff can and does break down and then where are you?' said Angel. 'I'd rather rely on old-fashioned seamanship.'

He smiled at her. It was the first time she had seen him smile and it wrought an extraordinary change on features which in repose and when his expression was serious suggested a forceful but somewhat stern personality. Suddenly charm was evident; a great deal of charm.

'I agree,' he said unexpectedly. 'I shouldn't care to put my trust in a skipper without the old skills of hand and eye as a back-up to the latest gadgets.' He turned to look at the sloop again. 'A few years ago, on a trip to America, I was taken to see the classic yacht regatta off Newport, Rhode Island. The Coup d'Elégance was won by a ketch built at Fife in Scotland way back in 1929. *Sea Fever* has the same beautiful lines. I'd like to see her under sail.'

Warmed by his praise, she said, 'You probably will . . . when I leave.'

'Where were you heading for before you stopped off here?' asked Leonora.

Her hand was no longer on Charles's arm. Within seconds of her placing it there, he had put his hand over hers, patted it and put it aside in a manner which suggested that, however intimate their private relationship might be, he disliked possessive caresses being bestowed on him in public.

'We were going to Java and from there to the east coast of Malaysia, but our plans were always fairly elastic.'

'I'm going for my swim,' said Charles. 'Ask Leonora what she would do in your position, Angel. She might not look like a career woman at the moment, but in fact she's a partner in a very successful public relations agency and is therefore an excellent person to advise you about your future.'

He rose to his feet and strode away.

Her tawny eyes following his tall figure, Leonora said, 'Charles's idea of a swim is a thirty-minute thrash which I find exhausting to watch. He has incredible energy, both physical and mental. You were lucky to have him on hand when you needed help. He doesn't spend much time in Bali, but it's typical of him to learn the language and to have the necessary contacts to handle any emergency.'

'Oh, I thought he lived here . . . worked here.'

'Good heavens, no! This is just a holiday house where he spends a few weeks in winter and entertains people with whom he has business involvements. Unfortunately I get lumbered with the wives who, more often than not, are as boring as the two who are here at the moment. Not a thought in their heads which isn't related to their husbands, their children, their houses or their clothes,' said Leonora, with a shrug.

To Angel these seemed the natural preoccupations of middle-aged women. Her grandmother had married at nineteen and devoted the rest of her life to being a wife and mother. Angel's mother had been a probationer in the London teaching hospital where her father had been a medical student. She had continued nursing for a short time after their marriage but had given up when she was pregnant and never resumed her career.

'Where is Mr Thetford's base?' she asked.

'We live in London,' said Leonora.

It sounded as if they lived together, a couple in all but name. Angel wondered why they didn't make it official. She could think of a number of possible reasons. They might think marriage archaic. Leonora was about the same age as Charles; one or both of them might have been married before and still have a partner in the background, or a divorce which put them off marrying again. Or maybe one of them wanted to marry but the other didn't. In which case probably it was Leonora who did and Charles who didn't. From what she had seen of him so far, Angel felt that he was a man who, if he wanted something, would move heaven and earth to get it.

She was about to ask about the public relations agency when the manservant came to enquire if there was anything more he could get for them.

'Some more coffee, please,' said Leonora. 'I have breakfast in bed when I'm here,' she added, when he had gone. 'Charles always gets up at six wherever he is, but he tries not to disturb me. There he goes now...and Gilbert with him. God, imagine going to bed with that barrel of lard!'

She was speaking of the Englishman who had sympathised with Angel the night before. Now, clad only in bathing trunks, he did not look his best, especially when his portly body, too white-fleshed to acquire a sun-tan easily and quickly, was seen next to Charles's long brown limbs and flat midriff as the two men continued down the beach after discarding their thongs and dropping their towels beside them.

Charles entered the water at a run, flinging himself forward in a plunge-dive from which he surfaced seconds later, shaking his head and raking back his wet hair, his raised arm gleaming like bronze. Gilbert waded to waist-depth before starting a leisurely breast stroke.

'See you later!' they heard Charles call before he rolled like a seal and struck out in the direction of the headland, his head low in the water, his arms rising and falling in the effortless rhythm of a born swimmer.

Seeing him made Angel aware that both yesterday and the day before she had missed her morning and evening swims. Normally they were as much a part of her daily routine as brushing her teeth and combing the long sun-bleached hair which fell in a heavy swathe down her back almost down to her waist. When, sometimes, she wore it plaited, it could be seen that the colour, in a temperate climate, would have been medium brown. Her eyebrows and lashes were dark brown, the lashes fringing a pair of large, wide-apart eyes with irises of the deep, vivid blue which Ludovic Dorset's eyes must have been when he was a young man.

The coffee came and with it another pot of fragrant Balinese tea for Angel.

'Mr Thetford thinks I should sell up and go to England, but I don't know anyone there and I think I'd be a fish out of water,' she said.

Leonora asked her much the same questions he had asked. After hearing the answers, she said,

'Australia would be more your scene than Europe, I should think. If you've lived out here virtually all your life, you'd shrivel in an English winter. Also, with no qualifications, you'd have a hard time getting a job. It seems to me a more practical idea is to sell the boat, spend some of the money on a training course and invest the rest to give you a small basic income. I'm sure Charles could give you some introductions to people in Sydney. He has contacts all over the world.'

'He mentioned an interest in satellite navigation. What's his principal interest?' asked Angel.

'He's a corporate consultant with Cornwall Chester, the most aggressive merchant bankers in the City...the City of London,' Leonora added explanatorily. 'Do you know what a merchant bank is? Basically, instead of handling money and loans for ordinary people and small firms like the high street banks, merchant banks deal with million-aires' money, large corporations and institutions, even governments. They handle takeover bids and arrange issues of shares...in other words, high finance.'

'He doesn't look like a banker...or not my idea of a banker,' said Angel, her eyes on the man who, having swum to the headland, was now re-crossing the bay, slicing through the water as if power-driven.

'No, Gilbert is more in line with most people's image of a banker, but in fact a lot of the younger financiers take fitness seriously...they have to, to stand the pace,' said Leonora. 'It's a tough life, wheeling and dealing...which is why Charles needs to relax when he's here and not get too involved in other people's problems,' she added meaningly.

'Don't worry, Miss York. I have no intention of asking Mr Thetford for any more help than he's already given me. As soon as my clothes are ready—which they may be by now—I'll move on.'

Angel hadn't intended to leave today, but in view of the pointed hint it seemed best to depart forthwith.

'There's no need for that,' said Leonora. 'Stay for lunch...talk to the others...ask their advice. But I think Charles probably underestimates your ability to do your own thing. After knocking about the East with your grandfather for years, you have to be a lot more canny than most girls of eighteen. Perhaps you can find another girl to crew for you. Plenty of girls learn to sail these days. Look at the number of women who've done long voyages single-handed.'

'It's a possibility,' Angel agreed. 'If you'll excuse me, I'll go and see about my clothes.'

She left the gazebo and walked purposefully back to the house. It was obvious that Leonora didn't want her around, although why she should feel that way was inexplicable. Perhaps it was that she only liked men and was bored not merely by the two wives staying here but by the entire female sex. Angel had read about women who prided themselves on being 'men's women'. But it seemed a curious attitude in someone who had chosen public relations as a career. Not that Angel was very clear what public relations involved.

She *had* known about merchant banks, because Ludo had acted for some of them in cases before the High Court in his years as a barrister. She had rather resented the patronising tone of Leonora's explanation. The fact was that she and Charles's girlfriend had instinctively disliked each other on sight, but why that should be so perplexed her.

In the house she met Lila, who said her own clothes weren't ready yet. As they were her best clothes anyway, Angel decided to row out to the sloop, change into her bikini, have a quick swim, then put on a T-shirt and shorts and come back ashore with the borrowed clothes. By that time Charles would have finished his swim and she could say goodbye and be on her way to an anchorage closer to Kuta. On that side of the island the sea wasn't calm as it was here; it swept ashore in huge combers, ideal for surfing. She would probably berth off Sanur, another of the main tourist areas, and go to Kuta by mini-bus. Transport was no problem in the more populated parts of the island.

Returning to where she had beached the rubber dinghy, she was puzzled to find the oars missing. Who could have taken them? Anywhere else she might have thought they had been stolen, but not here on what was virtually a private beach. Could they have been removed to a place of safe keeping by an over-cautious servant?

'Good morning, Miss Dorset. We met briefly last night. I'm Gilbert Winterton.' His stout body swathed in a towelling beach robe, the Englishman offered his hand. A double line of footprints in the damp sand at the sea's edge showed that after his swim he had been for a stroll.

'Good morning,' she said. 'My oars have vanished. I hope they haven't been pinched.'

'No, no, Charles has them somewhere,' he told her. 'He was carrying them when I met him in the garden this morning. Perhaps he thought it unwise to leave them lying about. I don't know what he did with them. Gave them to one of the staff, I expect. He was only gone a few moments and then he came back and we walked down here together. Gloriously warm, the sea here. I'm a bit like a hippopotamus... enjoy a nice wallow but never was much of a swimmer. But, my word, you should see Thetford go! He's still out there somewhere.' He shaded his eyes with his hand, scanning the sea. 'Where's he got to? Can you spot him?'

Angel was accustomed to squinting at the sea through narrowed eyes, but she couldn't see any sign of Charles.

'Where the devil has he got to?' said Gilbert, with a hint of anxiety. 'Seems to have vanished, like your oars. I say I hope he's all right. Even strong swimmers can get cramp.'

CHAPTER THREE

'THERE aren't sharks in these waters, are there?' was Gilbert's next question.

There was definite alarm in his voice now. Angel guessed that he was a man who, deep down, was afraid of the sea and whose subconscious fears were quickly brought to the surface in circumstances such as this.

She also felt some misgivings, but not because she thought anything bad had happened to Charles.

'Don't worry, Mr Winterton. Look, there he is ... on board our boat.'

It came as no great surprise to her to see Charles stepping on to the deck from the main hatchway. She hadn't locked up when they came ashore after her grandfather's burial. She had gone below for a moment to replace the key without which the engine couldn't be started on the hook in the saloon where it was kept when not in use. It had always been Ludo who had pocketed the sloop's keys when they went ashore together; and this morning, upset and preoccupied, she hadn't thought it necessary to lock up for the short time she had expected to be ashore.

Charles didn't linger on *Sea Fever*'s deck but swung long legs over her rails and dived neatly into the sea, his take-off causing the sloop to rock gently at her moorings.

'Well, that's a relief,' said Gilbert. 'For a moment he had me worried, disappearing like that.' He turned to her. 'You're going to be staying with us for a bit, I gather, Miss Dorset... getting your bearings after this sad event.'

'Did Mr Thetford tell you that?' she asked, her misgivings increasing.

He nodded. 'No doubt it would have been a great relief to your grandfather had he known that, by a fortunate chance, his... er... demise occurred at a place where the help and support of compatriots was not far to seek.'

Angel said nothing. She was beginning to find Mr Winterton irritating. How Ludo would have snorted at that euphemistic 'demise'! And what made this overweight banker suppose that compatriots were necessarily the best people to help her?

Lila, who had wiped her tears away so tenderly in the bathroom this morning, would never have said what Leonora had said on the terrace last night. If Angel had been obliged to go to the village for aid, doubtless they would have been just as helpful. Kindness and sympathy were not the prerogative of Europeans, as his tone seemed to imply.

She watched Charles swim back to the beach. As he stood up and waded ashore, water streaming from his powerful shoulders, she saw that against his bronzed chest lay a small tube-shaped container on a cord, a container in which he might, on occasion, carry a car key and money. As he couldn't possibly need either of those things here, the tube must contain something else—her keys.

While his girlfriend was anxious to see the back of her as soon as possible, was Charles proposing to keep her here by force?

'Why have you taken my oars away?' she asked, as he joined them.

'Do you want them?'

'Yes, please. I'd like to swim and my bathing suit's on board.'

'Why not borrow a bikini from my wife—she's brought at least half a dozen—and I know she'd be happy to lend you one. Save you rowing out to the boat,' suggested the older man.

'Thank you, but I'd rather not bother her.' Angel looked up at Charles. 'Where are the oars?'

'I'll fetch them for you. It won't take long.' He moved away to pick up his towel and rubber thongs.

Watching him rinse his feet in the pool inside the balustrade, she wondered if she might be mistaken and he hadn't taken her keys. But what other reason could he have had for boarding the sloop?

She had dragged the light dinghy to the water's edge by the time he returned, his wet trunks replaced by cotton shorts, his broad chest still bare, the tube no longer hanging from his neck.

Angel hitched up her borrowed skirt so that it wouldn't get wet and together they floated the dinghy.

'Hop in,' said Charles. He still had the short, lightweight oars balanced on his shoulder.

She obeyed, thinking he would hand them to her one by one. But the next moment he was in the dinghy with her and obviously intending to do the rowing.

As she opened her mouth to protest that this wasn't necessary, he said, 'While I was swimming I was thinking things over. I have a suggestion to make. By the way, it occurred to me that you hadn't locked up, so I came aboard, as you saw, found the keys and locked the door to the hatchway. At times we've had three or four cruising yachts in this bay and on one occasion a guest of mine had a pair of expensive sunglasses stolen from the beach, so one can't be too careful.'

Relieved that it was only security-consciousness which had made him remove the oars and the keys, she said, 'I should have locked up myself, but I'm still . . . a bit off course. What's your suggestion?'

'Have your swim first. While you're doing that I'll make some coffee and then we'll discuss my idea.'

'All right,' she agreed.

Sea Fever had more accommodation between decks than the sleekness her hull suggested. There were two double cabins, two singles, heads and showers fore and aft with a roomy saloon amidships and a well-designed galley. In addition there was plenty of locker space and an alcove fitted with a chart table.

Within a few minutes of boarding, Angel was in her bikini, diving into water as clear and shining as a fine aquamarine held under a strong light. She had not showed Charles where things were kept in the galley but left him to look for himself. It would be interesting to see if a man accustomed to dealing with vast sums of money could cope with something as simple as making coffee in unfamiliar surroundings.

Long ago, while teaching her to gut and fillet a fish, her grandfather had described his discovery, in middle age, that he couldn't perform the simple tasks of washing, ironing and mending his clothing and cooking appetising meals. All his life, up to that time, he had been waited on by women and never realised how helpless he was without them.

'And it took me quite a long time to learn how to look after myself,' he had added. 'If Eva hadn't died I might have gone to my grave not knowing how to sew on a button or knock up a decent omelette.'

In his seventies his skill with a needle was such that often he would pass the evenings doing needle-point while Angel read aloud. The wife of an American yachtsman had introduced him to cushions, or pillows as she had called them, with succinct slogans embroidered on them. Ludo's last piece of canvaswork had been a cushion cover with the slogan *I fight poverty—I work*.

Remembering, as she swam, their evenings together—good coffee, a good cigar and a glass of good brandy after the main meal of the day were three things which Ludo had retained from his previous way of life— Angel felt as if the bottom had dropped out of her world. To combat the pain of loss, she flung herself into a fast racing crawl.

She felt better for the vigorous swim. The fragrance of freshly ground, newly percolated coffee was wafting from below when she swung herself up the boarding ladder. Charles came on deck at the same moment that she gathered her streaming hair into a hank to squeeze some of the water from it.

Her body wasn't as brown as his because in a
temperate climate her skin would have been paler
than the naturally olive pigmentation which went
with his almost black hair. Nor did she ever lie in
the sun like people who lived in colder parts of the
world and wanted to soak up as much sun as possible. Not while they had been at sea but whenever
they were moored, Ludo had rigged up an awning
to shade the afterdeck. So although she had lived
in the sun for thirteen years and had only small
areas of flesh which had never been exposed to it,
her tan was a deep golden colour, not the leather-
brown look acquired by tourists who came to the
East for two or three weeks of dedicated sun-
worship.

When Charles looked at her, for the first time in
her life she was aware of being almost naked. His
appraisal was brief and impersonal, which in itself
made her conscious that her figure left a lot to be
desired. Up to now she had never minded having
small breasts and no other curves to speak of. Suddenly she longed to be more rounded and less leggy.
A twenty-inch waist was an asset only if it were
combined with full breasts and hips, which in her
case it wasn't.

While he returned to the galley to bring the coffee
on deck, she wrapped a sarong round herself. When
Charles came back, the two parts of her bikini were
draped over the rails to dry and from chest to knee
she was swathed in indigo-on-pale-ochre cotton, like
a Balinese girl going to the river for a bath.

He had even found the biscuit tin, she noticed,
with a tightening of the throat. She and her grandfather had taken it in turns to bake bread, but he

had kept the biscuit tin filled because he had a sweet tooth. Angel's mother had wanted her to have beautiful teeth and as a small child she had been given pieces of carrot and apple in place of sweets. By the time she had come to live with Ludo her taste had been formed. She loved fruit, especially ripe papaya with its beautiful dawn-sky flesh, but anything made with refined sugar tasted sickly to her. At eleven and four, while her grandfather ate biscuits or cake, she had had a small sweet banana or a slice of pineapple. ·

While she was in the water, Charles had not only made coffee, he had set up the two deckchairs which, at sea, were kept lashed to the hatch cover. Perhaps, unlike Ludo in his younger days, Charles had not been waited on hand and foot by women. Angel wondered if he were what her grandfather had termed a self-made man, or if he had started life from a privileged position. He had certainly been born with every physical advantage, she thought, watching the play of muscle from broad shoulder to shapely hand as he poured out the coffee he'd made.

'I've been thinking for some time that I'd like to have a boat,' he said. 'There's something about this one which appeals to me. If a survey shows she's basically sound, I'm prepared to buy a half-share in her and to finance a refit. That would enable you to keep her *and* take a training course of some kind. What I should want in return for my investment would be the use of her for myself and my guests from November to February. How does that strike you?'

As she knew roughly what a refit would be likely to cost, it struck her as amazingly generous—too generous.

'I should have to think about it,' she said cautiously.

'Naturally. What I've given you is only the outline of the arrangement. We should have to thrash out the details. And the whole thing is contingent on a qualified marine surveyor giving her a thorough check, but that shouldn't be difficult to arrange.'

He leaned back in his chair, his long legs stretched out in front of him and crossed at the ankle, giving her time to think about it while he watched with narrowed eyes a triangular-sailed Balinese fishing boat with outriggers heading out to sea.

'I'm not too happy about the idea of selling a half-share,' said Angel, after some reflection. 'I think sixty-forty, in my favour, would be more acceptable. After all, you know nothing about boats...or not much. It makes sense for the person who knows how to sail her to have the final say if a difference of opinion arises.'

He looked at her thoughtfully. She wondered what was in his mind. She and Ludo had shared an almost telepathic understanding of each other's thought processes. Maybe it was because they had only just met that Charles seemed enigmatic, no hint of his thoughts showing in his expression.

'All right, I'll agree to that on condition that you agree to come to England for a year,' was his unexpected reply. 'It will take at least that long to spruce her up, I should imagine, and it will be a good opportunity for you to see how the other half of the world lives. I have an aunt with a house in London which is far too big for her. I'm sure she'll be pleased to put you up while you find your feet.'

'I don't understand your concern for my welfare, Mr Thetford,' she began. 'I——'

'Call me Charles,' he cut in. 'And my concern for your welfare is no more than any responsible person would feel for a young girl left in your circumstances. It's obvious that your life with your grandfather has to some extent kept you isolated from the pressures and influences on most girls of your age group. You're in a vulnerable position and there are men who would try to take advantage of that. But I'm not one of them. Disabuse yourself of the idea that I have any sinister designs on you.'

Angel flushed. 'I'm sure you haven't. I wasn't suggesting that you had. It's just that most people are so busy with their own lives that they haven't time to bother with other people's difficulties. And your life sounds busier than most.'

Charles arched an eyebrow. 'What do you know about my life?'

'Only what I can see and what Miss York mentioned. You're obviously very rich and...and high-powered.'

He gave a short laugh. 'Rich is a relative term, and what does high-powered mean? I work harder than most people. I don't have a wife or children or any absorbing interests other than my work. To be successful in my world—which is very different from your world—it's only necessary to put one's whole heart and back into something, but not many people do that. They prefer to fritter their energies on half a dozen things. Business, like art, demands total dedication.'

'And is it as satisfying as art, do you think?'

'I find it extremely satisfying. If I didn't I should do something else.' As he spoke he glanced at his watch and uncrossed his ankles, drawing in his legs and rising to his feet in the manner of someone who has idled long enough.

'I have things to do. I suggest you spend the rest of the morning thinking over my proposition. If you decide to go for it, after lunch, while the others are resting, we'll work out the details.'

As he had before they took off from Bali, earlier this morning, on the first lap of the flight, the first-class cabin steward came round again with a basket of small hand towels which had been plunged in boiling water and wrung out. They were still hot, damp and refreshing. Next came the stewardess with crystal goblets of ice-cold orange juice.

Angel, who had the window seat on the starboard side of the aisle with the adjoining seat empty, wondered if the economy-class passengers were also being given hot towels and cold juice. Having seen them, a short time ago, crowded into a large public lounge while the first-class passengers had an air-conditioned private lounge, she was inclined to doubt it.

They were at the airport of Jakarta, the capital of Indonesia, and very soon would be taking off for Bangkok where they would be staying for two nights because Charles had business there.

He and Leonora were occupying the pair of seats on the opposite side of the aisle. Leonora was trying

on a pair of earrings she had bought, or he had
bought for her, in the jeweller's shop in the airport.

Exploring the small shopping complex, Angel
had noticed that everything on sale seemed to be
much more expensive than in ordinary shops. She
had seen nothing she wanted to buy.

It had surprised her that Amy and Maureen, who
had done a lot of shopping in Bali, should want to
add to their purchases at this airport. They and their
husbands were still in the glass-walled first-class
lounge, waiting for their flights to Los Angeles and
Hong Kong to be called. Shopping seemed to be a
passion with them. Angel had been astonished when
she'd seen the number of suitcases they had brought
for their holiday at Charles's house. Two porters
with trolleys had been needed to handle all the
baggage. Only she and Charles travelled light, he
with a thing called a suit bag and an expensive-
looking flight bag, and she with one medium-sized
case stamped with Ludo's initials and containing
her few clothes and her favourite books.

Leonora, on seeing the case, had said it should
be thrown out and replaced with a new one. Angel
had argued that although it looked a bit battered
it was still serviceable. At that time she hadn't realised that they would be flying first-class and her
case would look out of place amid piles of luxurious matched luggage. It didn't matter to her and
she didn't think it bothered Charles, but perhaps
it was an embarrassment to the others, especially
Leonora who, plainly, wouldn't have been pleased
to have Angel travelling with them even with a
brand new suitcase.

On Charles's advice, Angel's most precious possessions, the photograph of her parents, an album of snaps taken during the years with her grandfather, and his private logs as distinct from *Sea Fever*'s log books, were packed in the smart flight bag issued by the airline and now stowed in an overhead locker by one of the attentive stewardesses.

Suspecting that one paid a great deal of money for all this deferential cosseting, she would have been perfectly happy to travel in the cheaper part of the plane and rejoin the others on arrival at their destination. But Charles had booked her flight without consulting her, and obviously as far as he was concerned there was only one class—first.

Listening to Leonora and the other two women chatting while his party went through the formalities of departure, Angel had the impression they found travelling by air a great bore, having done it so often before.

For herself, having little or no memory of the flight she had made with Ludo when he had been summoned to Europe to take charge of her, this journey was, in effect, her first view of the world from the air and as such tremendously exciting. Today it would take only hours to reach the Gulf of Siam, instead of the weeks they had once spent getting there by sea.

She had been eleven that year, poised on the brink of adolescence. Tim, their crew, had been eighteen, a man in some ways, a youth in others. She had almost forgotten about him until looking through the photograph album for the first time in a long while she had come across a snap Ludo had taken from the deck while Tim was rowing her ashore to buy some supplies they needed.

Tim was also mentioned several times in the detailed record of events kept by her grandfather in addition to the factual logs.

> Tim Bolton, great-nephew of my old friend and colleague, John Bolton, came aboard. A well-built, well-mannered youngster but not happy, according to John who asked me to give him a berth for a couple of months. Parents divorced. Father seriously displeased that the boy has failed to qualify for Sandhurst.

A couple of weeks later, Ludo had written:

> Tim has settled down well and does more than pull his weight. He's intelligent, reliable, has a strong sense of humour and would, in my opinion, have made a first-rate officer. However, if O and A levels are more important than qualities of character in the modern Army, that's their loss. I feel sure he'll do well when he finds his métier. Angel, dubious of him at first, now shows every sign of developing a crush.

Had she had a crush on Tim? Angel wondered, as the aircraft taxied out to the main runway. If so it must have worn off very quickly after he had gone back to Europe. He would be twenty-five now. She wondered if he *had* found his métier. He hadn't kept in touch and shortly after his voyage with them his great-uncle John, a judge who had once been in chambers with Ludo, had died. Ludo had only found that out by chance, coming across a reference to 'the late Sir John Bolton Q.C.' in an out-of-date periodical in a yacht club. What had become of Tim they...*she* would never know.

How hard it was to stop the habit of thinking of herself as half of a partnership, she thought, with a sigh. This was how widows must feel...bereft. She didn't remember grieving for her parents, although she must have missed them deeply at the time. But now, after losing Ludo, every so often a great wave of pain and loneliness would sweep over her, making her want to hide in a corner and cry.

The steward and stewardess reappeared, this time with glasses of champagne to sip while the plane was taking off and a large silver tray of delicious-looking titbits served, when each passenger had made their selection, on a gold-rimmed plate decorated with an orchid and accompanied by a linen napkin.

Angel remembered an adage she had once read, something about money not buying happiness but enabling one to be miserable in comfort!

She glanced across the aisle at the other two. Leonora was flicking through a fashion magazine bought at the airport. Charles was studying some kind of report which had come through on his Telex machine and jotting notes in the margins.

She wondered if she had done the right thing in agreeing to his proposition and selling him a substantial share in *Sea Fever*.

CHAPTER FOUR

ALTHOUGH she had visited the southern part of Thailand before, Angel had never been to Bangkok, or indeed to any large city. Ludo had avoided them, preferring small fishing ports to the crowded and expensive marinas of large ones.

'The Thai name for Bangkok is Krung Thep—City of Angels,' Charles told her, as a large air-conditioned limousine swept them away from the airport some way outside the city. 'At first sight the downtown area isn't attractive. I'm told it was in the old days, before the canals were filled in. Everything went by waterway then. Now Bangkok is choked by road traffic and the noise and the fumes are hellish. But if you know where to look, the old charm still lingers in places.'

To Angel, the crowded streets were fascinating and she actually enjoyed a succession of traffic jams because they gave her more chance to look at the buildings and the people. But Leonora tapped impatient fingers on the cover of her glossy magazine and visibly fumed with annoyance when a man in a dilapidated van peered at the occupants of the big car stopped alongside him as if they were unusual animals in a cage at the zoo. His uninhibited interest made Angel repress a grin, and she was glad to see Charles's mouth twitch slightly.

Poor Leonora, she thought. It was rather hard on her if she had expected to come to Bangkok alone with him and now found herself saddled with an unwanted third party. Angel could understand the older woman's feelings even if, in her place, out of politeness and kindness she would have tried not to show how unwelcome an interloper was.

Perhaps Leonora's lack of sensitivity to Angel's feelings was caused by her own deep unhappiness because she suspected that Charles was never going to marry her. At least, he hadn't sounded as if marriage was on his agenda the day he had talked about business demanding total dedication.

'Do you have a dress in your case, Angel?' he asked suddenly.

'No, I haven't,' she answered. 'I've never really needed one. The only parties I've been to have always been on boats, where my jeans were OK.'

'Not all restaurants look favourably on jeans. You'd better buy a dress for dinner tonight. Leonora will help you choose something suitable.'

'I shan't have time, Charles,' said Leonora. 'As soon as we arrive I want to have my hair and my nails done. Angel doesn't have to eat in the restaurant tonight. She can have dinner in her room and watch a video movie on television. That will be far more of a treat for her, won't it, Angel?'

As an affirmative answer was clearly what was required of her, Angel was about to agree when Charles said, 'I should think it would bore her witless. She hasn't been reared on a diet of soap operas and second-rate movies. If you're too busy, I'll go shopping with her. It won't take more than half an hour.'

For an instant Leonora looked furious. 'She might prefer to go shopping on her own. She's not a child.'

Charles made no response to this and Angel judged it best to hold her tongue. It made her uncomfortable to be the cause of strife between them. Although it was possible there had been some latent discord before she appeared on the scene.

Fortunately it wasn't long before the car arrived at their hotel. At the reception desk in the enormous lobby Charles was greeted as if he had stayed there many times before. Soon they were being ushered into a lift by someone who looked as if he might be the manager of this super-de-luxe place or, if not the manager, his deputy.

'We've given you your usual suite, Mr Thetford, and Miss Dorset's room is on the floor below,' said this personage.

When the lift stopped and the bellboy accompanying them stepped out to take Angel to her room, Charles said to the manager, 'Miss York has some urgent appointments and wants to unpack as soon as possible. I'll stop off here and make sure Miss Dorset understands how everything works.'

The door unlocked by the bellboy led into a bedroom which made Angel's eyes widen at its opulence. An open door gave a glimpse of an equally luxurious private bathroom. But it was the view through the expanse of glass that formed the outer wall of the room which really took her breath away. The large window looked down on a broad river which she knew must be the Chao Phraya, where on special occasions the golden royal barges with their crews of scarlet-uniformed oarsmen rowed past.

'What a fabulous view!' she said eagerly. 'Who needs television with an outlook like this? I'll be perfectly happy having my supper on a tray and watching the river traffic.'

'You will eat with us,' said Charles firmly. He showed her how to control the air-conditioning and checked that the shower over the bath was simple to operate.

'These robes are for guests to wear going to and from the swimming pool in the garden,' he explained. The room had twin beds, enough towels for six people, it seemed to Angel, and two terry robes hanging on the back of the bathroom door. 'As soon as they bring your case up, why don't you get out your bikini and go down and have a swim. I'll meet you in the lobby in an hour and we'll go shopping.'

'Charles, it really isn't necessary for you to come with——' she began.

'Possibly not,' he cut in. 'You may have an instinctively good dress sense, or you may need to learn it. Be downstairs in an hour.'

Waiting for Charles in the lobby—she was there before the appointed time—reminded Angel of the man who had gawked at them in the traffic jam. Although she gazed more discreetly, she was no less fascinated by the hotel guests coming and going through the lobby with its shining marble floor, cascading chandeliers and elaborate arrangements of flowers.

The glass doors were opened for them by a white-gloved young doorman who was also wearing white stockings with the *panung*, a garment not unlike a sarong but drawn up between the legs to give a re-semblance to knickerbockers. She knew its name because among the books she was taking with her to Europe was one on the traditional costumes of the peoples of South-East Asia which had been her fourteenth birthday present from her grandfather.

Darling Ludo! Each time she thought of him, it was with that sinking sense of loss. To stop herself lapsing into unhappiness, she began to play a game he had taught her when she was small.

She had been playing it for some minutes when she sensed that someone was watching her and looked round to find Charles standing a few yards away, his hands in the pockets of a pair of the light-weight trousers Americans called chinos.

Going towards him, she said, 'I'm sorry...I didn't see you there. Why didn't you speak?'

'I was trying to work out what was going on in your mind,' he answered. 'For several minutes your expression has been alternating between a slight smile and a slight frown.'

'Has it? How idiotic I must have looked! I was playing Ludo's game,' Angel explained. 'It's better to play it with someone else and score points, but you can play it by yourself. You have to predict what people will do. What language they will speak if they're foreigners. What they'll choose from the menu. What they'll drink in a bar. Whether they're smokers or non-smokers—that sort of thing.'

'I see. What were you predicting about the people arriving?' he asked.

'Three things; whether they'd smile at the doorman, say thank you, or ignore him.'

'I see, and how was your score?'

'Not good. I expected people staying in a place like this to have better manners than they seem to have—at least judging by that sample. Perhaps the next ten people to come through the door will be more courteous,' she said hopefully.

'I doubt it.' His tone was cynical. 'I've held doors open myself—in London, New York and Madrid—and could have remained there all day for all the notice anyone took. I've no doubt professional doormen get used to being ignored and aren't bothered by it as much as you are.'

'Perhaps not, but who can tell what effects small rudenesses have? Perhaps it's an apocryphal story, but they say that Ho Chi Minh became a Communist, defeating the French and later supporting the Viet-Cong, because he was treated with contempt when he lived in England and France as a young man.'

'There may be an element of truth in it. Shall we go?'

When the doorman opened the door for her, Angel smiled and said, *'Khawp, khun,'* part of the basic Thai which she and Tim Bolton had picked up long ago. According to her grandfather, any civilised person learnt to say please and thank you in the language of the country they were visiting.

The doorman's impassive expression changed to a grin. 'You're welcome.'

Evidently he took them for Americans!

'Did you have a swim?' Charles enquired, as they crossed the hotel's forecourt where several uniformed drivers were waiting beside gleaming cars like the one which brought them from the airport.

'Yes, I did—and used the dryer in the bathroom to dry my hair. Tonight I'm going to have a long lying-down bath. There's even a little pillow, with suckers, to rest one's head on.... and a face cloth ... and wonderful *thick* towels, as good as the towels at your house. I didn't realise how thin and scratchy our towels were until I used yours and the hotel's. How much does a room here cost?'

'Less than it would in London, because wages are lower here. No, thank you, we're walking——' this to a hopeful taxi-driver.

Not far from the hotel they came to a major thoroughfare where Charles took her by the arm and hurried her across the road during a gap in the traffic. Angel concluded, from his purposeful stride, that he knew where he was going. Perhaps on a previous visit he had shopped with Leonora. It wasn't yet clear from their conversation how long they had been together.

A few minutes later they climbed the steps of an expensive-looking shop called Design Thai.

'May I help you?' A small, slender girl, her lustrous black hair cut in the pageboy style worn, Angel had noticed, by many Thai girls, smiled enquiringly at them.

'We're looking for a simple dress to wear in the evening. The plainer the better,' said Charles.

'What size?' the salesgirl asked, looking at Angel.

'I'm not sure.'

The assistant cast an experienced eye over her figure. 'I show you what we have. This way, please.'

She led them to a rail of silk dresses. 'I think this your size.' She selected a pale pink frock with embroidery on the sleeves and round the hem.

Before Angel could make any comment, Charles said decisively, 'Too fussy. What about the blue one?'

'That one also right size . . . very nice,' the salesgirl agreed.

When she took it from the rail to display it, he gave a nod of approval.

'Go and try it on.'

Somewhat stung by his authoritative manner, as if he were talking to a child, Angel did as she was told. But once the blue dress was on, she knew that his judgement was right. The silk matched the blue of her eyes and the style with its full skirt and tight waist suited her coltish figure. The neckline was modestly low at the front and more daring at the back, but a short matching jacket fastened by loops and Turk's head knots turned it into an outfit which could be worn during the day for a formal occasion. But her life had never included formal occasions, and would it ever?

'Excellent,' was Charles's verdict, when she emerged from the fitting-room and showed herself to him. In her absence he had cast his eye over the rest of the shop's stock and picked out a skirt and two blouses which were being held by another assistant. 'Now go and try these on.'

The skirt was made of navy blue cotton, both blouses were white, one with a sailor's collar trimmed with navy blue braid and the other with a rounded collar and tucks down the front. Both made her look very young, like a schoolgirl, she thought.

Charles didn't ask her opinion. He said briskly, 'We'll take them.' By the time she re-emerged from the fitting-room, the clothes had been packed in a carrier and he was paying for them.

'Now you need shoes,' he said, as they left the shop and continued along the busy street. 'The girl who served us has recommended a place which isn't far.'

'I'm sure I could manage to buy some shoes by myself if you only have half an hour to spare.'

'I've rearranged my appointments. I'm in no hurry. In England it will be cold and you'll need warmer clothes, but the summer isn't far off, so we may as well get you kitted out with some lighter things. You may have filled out by then, but I don't think you're ever going to suffer from puppy fat,' he remarked, with a downward glance at her slender figure.

In the shoe shop, the assistant brought high heels for her to try, but Charles frowned and shook his head.

'You have pretty feet. Don't spoil them by cramming them into tight shoes and tottering around on stilt heels,' he told her. 'When I notice a woman walking gracefully, invariably she's barefoot or next to barefoot—never in fashionable shoes.'

Angel didn't mind his prohibition on high heels, but she queried his insistence on a colour called taupe which turned out to be what she would have described as muddy river water.

'Why this colour? Why not blue to match the dress?' she asked, as the assistant gave her a nylon stocking to put on her bare brown foot before trying on the plain low-heeled style which Charles had specified.

'Because a woman who travels the world and always looks elegant told me that if there's only room for one pair of shoes in a suitcase this is what they should be, taupe pumps...what in England are called court shoes.'

'Did she explain why?'

'No, but having seen how little baggage she takes around with her, and how good she looks, I take her word for it. She has more claim to be on the list of the world's best-dressed women than anyone with closets full of clothes which are only worn a few times,' he said drily.

Angel wondered who she was and how close their relationship had been. Surely a woman would only talk about clothes to a man with a strong interest in her? Otherwise she would be afraid of boring him.

After buying the shoes and a small taupe leather bag with a detachable leather strap which made it suitable for day or evening use, they walked back towards the river.

'You'll have to deduct what all these things cost from the price of your share of *Sea Fever*,' said Angel.

The sloop had been surveyed before they left Bali and he had made her an offer which she had accepted.

Near the hotel there was a shop with nightdresses and underwear in the window. Perhaps guessing that she slept in a sarong, Charles said, 'You'd better buy yourself some night things. I'll leave the choice of them to you.'

Having paid for everything else with a bank card, he opened his billfold and gave her some five-hundred-baht notes.

'I'll have these parcels sent to your room. Come up to the suite about seven.'

When Angel returned to her bedroom with another large carrier containing peach silk pyjamas piped with aquamarine and an aquamarine man's-style dressing gown piped with peach, the rest of the shopping was already there, with the addition of a package she hadn't seen before.

Puzzled, she removed the wrapping from a long narrow box which contained a string of small pearls and a pair of pearl earrings. There was also a card with a message in writing she recognised.

'An advance present for your eighteenth birthday.'

She was ready by a quarter to seven. As she looked at herself in the full-length mirror, she could see that she looked nice. But was this demure young person in blue silk and pearls the real Angel Dorset, or was she Charles's idea of how a girl of her age ought to look?

Perhaps it was only because she wasn't used to wearing a dress that she didn't feel herself, she thought, studying her reflection. Or maybe it was her hair which wasn't right. Long loose hair looked all right with cotton, but not with this lustrous Thai silk, which called for something more formal. She gathered her hair into a bunch, twisted it, coiled it high at the back of her head and surveyed the effect. Better. Much better. But she had neither the time nor the hairpins to put it up tonight. Tomorrow, if there was a chance, she would buy some pins and also some make-up. She had once had a lipstick, bought on impulse in a market and used for a few days until, left in the sun, it had melted into a gooey mess. She hadn't bothered to replace it.

It was a few seconds to seven when she pressed the bell beside the door of Charles's suite. It was only as she checked the time that she realised the man's watch she had automatically replaced on her wrist after her bath wasn't in keeping with the rest of her appearance. But as she hadn't brought the new bag with her, and the dress had no pockets, she had nowhere to put it if she took it off.

Charles opened the door. 'Spot on time,' he said, with a smile.

He was wearing a pale grey suit of some tropic-weight cloth, with a pink shirt and a grey tie striped diagonally with pink. As he stood aside for her to enter a mirrored lobby, she caught a faint spicy scent which might be his soap, shampoo or aftershave.

The lobby led into a large and luxurious sitting-room with two long, deep-cushioned sofas covered in pale green Thai silk to match the large celadon vases used as lamp-bases on the glass end-tables. There was no sign of Leonora.

'What would you like to drink? Orange juice...Coke...fresh lime juice?' Charles suggested.

Angel thought about asking for a Campari and soda, a deep pink drink she had heard being or-dered by a girl a year or two older than herself while she was at the pool earlier in the day. But she didn't know how strong it was, so she decided to play safe. 'Lime juice, please.'

As he moved across the room to an elaborate gilt side-table with a tray of drinks and glasses and a large ice bucket on it, she said, 'Thank you very much for the pearls. It's very kind and generous of you.'

'I noticed you had pierced ears. In America it's the custom, in traditionalist families, to give pearls to girls of eighteen.'

'Do you spend a lot of time in America?'

'Enough to find it worthwhile to keep a pied-à-terre there.' He handed her a tall glass and turned his cuff back from his watch. She saw his dark brows contract slightly before he picked up his own glass of what looked like gin and tonic. 'Come and sit down.'

They sat on opposite sofas. Had she been alone in the room, Angel would have slipped her feet out of her new shoes to delve her toes into the dense pile of the Chinese silk rug overlying the cream fitted carpet.

'How luxurious to have all this space,' she said, with a glance round the room. 'I was working out earlier on how many times my cabin on *Sea Fever* would fit into my bedroom here. Even the bathroom is larger.'

'How was your lying-down bath?' he asked, with a smile in his eyes.

'It was lovely. I might have another later on. A shower is fine for getting clean, but lying in a bath is better for thinking.'

'Have you been thinking about what to do with your time while the sloop is being refurbished?'

'Yes, and I've had two good ideas. First, I think I should——'

She stopped short as the sound of a door opening behind her distracted Charles's attention and made him rise to his feet.

A few minutes earlier she had sensed that he was annoyed because Leonora wasn't ready. No displeasure showed in his face now. He was looking over Angel's head with an expression which was as clear to her as his previous irritation; the expression of a man seeing a woman whose attractions outweigh her shortcomings.

Leonora closed the door behind her and strolled across to the sofas. She was wearing a knife-pleated skirt of dull black satin with buttons all down one side, most of them undone. A black satin jacket was draped over her shoulders. A glittering, gleaming gold halter top clung to her opulent breasts and was cinched at the waist by a wide and shiny black belt. In Bali she had been an outstandingly good-looking woman. Here in Bangkok, after several hours in a beauty parlour, she was a knockout.

'Hello, Angel. Don't you look sweet?' she said kindly. She turned to Charles. 'Am I going to be reprimanded for being five minutes late?' she asked, her tawny eyes teasing.

The next day Angel's lunch consisted of hot fritters and other tasty titbits from cooking stalls in the street. She actually found these cheap snacks, served on sticks or in paper cones, more enjoyable than last night's grand meal in the hotel restaurant.

Today she was supposed to be sightseeing and shopping with Leonora. That had been the plan settled last night, before Leonora had persuaded Charles to take her to a nightclub. But this morning, after he had left for the first of his meetings, Leonora had telephoned Angel and said, 'I have a migraine, so you'll have to look after yourself today. Take a guided tour round the temples—you can get details at the desk. I'm going to stay in bed. No, thanks, there's nothing you can do.'

A tour with a group of other tourists didn't appeal to Angel. She took a *tuk-tuk*, a three-wheeled open-sided vehicle with a noisy motor and room for two behind the driver, to the Grand Palace, a city within a city. After spending most of the morning there, she took another *tuk-tuk* to the heart of the Chinese quarter where she planned to spend the afternoon wandering around the crowded alleys and markets.

It was here that she had her lunch, confident that anything cooked in boiling fat must be as safe if not safer than the sauces and creamy puddings she had seen being served in the restaurant.

She had bought herself various cosmetics, some ribbons and combs for her hair and a pair of embroidered silk mules to wear with her new dressing-gown, when a voice said, 'Good afternoon.'

For a moment or two she didn't recognise the young Thai who was smiling at her. Then she realised it was the doorman who had said, 'You're welcome,' yesterday.

'You have been shopping, I see. Have you bought some nice things?' he asked. 'You're a long way from the hotel. Can you find your way back there? Perhaps you would like me to show you?'

Surprised at his excellent English, which she thought would have qualified him for a more interesting job than opening a door all day, Angel said, 'Are you on your way back to work?'

'No, not until later this evening, but I should be pleased to walk with you. I have nothing to do for the next hour, and talking to you would help to improve my English.'

'Your English seems perfect already.'

'No, no, it is very bad. You would be doing me a favour.'

'Where the hell have you been?'

Angel wasn't the only person who recoiled as Charles stepped out of the lift at lobby level where she was waiting to go up to her room.

Two other women flinched as the tall, angry man glared down at the startled girl.

'What was *that* all about, I wonder?' one of them said to her husband, after he had steered her round the palpably irate Englishman and the lift was on its way up again.

The white-haired American shrugged. 'Don't ask me, but I'd say she's in trouble. That guy sure was in a temper about something!'

CHAPTER FIVE

HIS strong fingers biting into her arm, Charles hustled Angel away from the busy area by the lifts.

'Where have you been?' he repeated, in a quieter part of the lobby. 'Leonora's been frantic! She was expecting you for lunch. When you didn't show up she didn't know what to do. By the time I came back at four she was going up the wall with worry.'

'I'm s-sorry,' Angel stammered. 'I meant to be back an hour ago, but I—I was delayed. Leonora and I must have got our wires crossed. I didn't realise she was expecting me back here for lunch. I thought if I came back at teatime it would be quite soon enough.'

'If she hadn't had one of her migraines, she wouldn't have let you out of her sight this morning,' he said curtly.

'I don't know why not ... I can cross the street by myself. I've been doing it for years.'

'Not in Bangkok you haven't. This town is famous for its brothels ... thinly disguised as massage parlours. There's more prostitution here than in any city in the East.'

'So there may be,' Angel retorted. 'But I've never heard that they abduct female tourists. The only man who's touched me today is you—and you're hurting my arm.'

'I'm sorry.' He released his grip. Still looking seriously displeased but no longer boiling over, he said curtly, 'The first thing to do is to let Leo know you're all right.'

They had the lift to themselves, but neither of them spoke. Angel knew she was at fault for arriving back after Charles instead of before him. In similar circumstances Ludo would have been annoyed with her. But he wouldn't have blazed at her in public, or grabbed her arm roughly enough to bruise it. He had never been a hot-tempered man, or never within her memory. But of course he had been old, half a century older than the tall tight-lipped man beside her.

By the time they stepped out of the lift into the luxuriously appointed corridor leading to the suites, she had pulled herself together and, but for one thing, would have been ready to explain and apologise. What stopped her saying she was sorry was Leonora's part in this upset. She had lied to Charles. She hadn't been expecting Angel to return at lunchtime, and nor had she been distraught with anxiety, or only to the extent that he would have blamed her if something bad had happened. In her heart she wouldn't have cared. To Charles's flamboyant girlfriend, Angel knew she was nothing but a nuisance.

The older woman was not in the sitting-room when they entered the suite. But the bedroom door was open, and Charles called out, 'It's all right . . . she's back. End of panic!'

He was on his way to the bedroom when Leonora appeared in the doorway. She was wearing a clinging green robe and no lipstick, which altered her appearance enough to make a man think she was pale and distraught. But her eyes were made up, Angel noticed. At dinner last night she had studied the way Leonora did her eyes and she could see that an equally skilful combination of shadows had been applied between her eyebrows and upper lashes today, with some shading under her lower lashes.

'Oh, what a relief! You're OK,' Leonora exclaimed. 'Where have you been, for God's sake? I've been biting my nails to the quick, imagining all kinds of horrors. It's really too bad of you, Angel! If you wanted to stay out all day, why didn't you leave a message? You must know how to use a pay-phone, don't you?'

Angel saw that she had two choices and must make a quick decision between them. She could contest Leonora's story about expecting her back for lunch, or she could let her get away with it. What would be gained by showing her up as a liar? Nothing. Charles might not believe the truth and having her veracity challenged would only make Leonora even more hostile. It was better to say nothing.

'I'm sorry if you were worried... but glad to see that your nail-biting was only metaphorical. It would have been a pity to spoil your nails on my account,' she said, with a glance at the long coral-varnished nails spread on Leonora's upper arms as she stood with her arms folded, a posture which also made the most of the eye-catching cleavage displayed in the V of the green robe.

Leonora's mouth thinned and her fingers curled, making her pointed nails look even more like shiny claws. 'You don't give a damn, you little——'

'Leo!' Charles cut in sharply.

For an instant the glare which had been focused on Angel was swivelled in his direction. Then she turned and stalked back to the bedroom, slamming the door.

Charles looked pained. 'You'd better go to your room,' he said, looking coldly at Angel. 'Perhaps when you join us for dinner tonight you'll have the grace to apologise properly.'

He didn't follow Leonora into the bedroom but crossed the room to the glass doors giving on to the suite's private terrace. Angel watched him go to the balustrade and stand with his hands on the top rail. She wondered if he was regretting taking her under his wing.

When, at a few minutes to seven, she made her way back to the suite, the mirrored walls of the lift showed several changes in the demure appearance they had reflected the night before.

Tonight she looked at least two years older, Angel thought, with satisfaction. Her hair was up, with a silver ribbon threaded through its coils. In place of the discreet pearl studs, silver earrings like crescent moons swung from the lobes of her ears, and her eyes and lips were carefully made up. She hadn't used as much paint as Leonora did because she knew it would look wrong on her. This time the lipstick she had bought wasn't a bright, hard red but a soft papaya-toned pink, and instead of choosing the blue shadow from the palette of six colours in her new eye make-up kit, she had used the merest dusting of green powder-shadow on her lids with dark blue mascara—but not much—brushed on her upper lashes. The idea for blueing her lashes had come from a close-up photograph of the Princess of Wales on the cover of a magazine someone had thrown away a couple of years ago and she had kept.

As she was walking along the corridor to Charles's suite, wondering how he and Leonora would react to her new look, she met an elderly couple leaving one of the other suites.

It seemed polite to smile and say good evening. A few moments later she was astonished to hear the woman say to her husband, 'Isn't that girl the image of Princess Di! For a moment I thought it was her.'

It had never occurred to Angel before, but perhaps, being tall and slender, with a similar bump on the bridge of her nose and cheeks which formed dimples when she grinned, she did bear a slight resemblance to the Princess. Especially now that her hair was up.

Cheered that someone could mistake her, even for a second, for the glamorous Diana, she pressed the door-bell.

This time it was Leonora who opened the door, but she didn't show any reaction to Angel's new look because she opened it without even checking that it was Angel who had rung.

Nor did Charles, who was fixing drinks, look round when Angel followed Leonora into the sitting-room.

It was only when she said, 'Charles has told me to apologise properly for upsetting you, Leonora,' that they both turned to look at her. 'If I really did worry you, then I beg your pardon,' she went on. 'I had no intention of being late. I was talking to someone interesting and didn't notice the time passing.'

Leonora's eyebrows had risen at the sight of the upswept hairdo and the earrings. Her expression as she took in the changes wasn't approving. What Charles thought it was impossible to tell.

'Who were you talking to?' he asked.

'One of the doormen...the young one. We met in a market in the Chinese quarter. His name is Cham. He grew up in a slum called Klong Toey. He was telling me about it, and also explaining the tones used in speaking Thai. He says it's difficult for Westerners to learn the correct tones because we put feelings—such as doubt or dislike—into our words. To speak Thai properly you must never allow any emotion to enter your voice.'

'And later on he offered to take you to a factory selling gemstones at wholesale prices, I suppose?' said Leonora.

'He never mentioned gemstones. Why should he?'

'Because that's the usual reason for Thais being friendly to foreigners. They're touting for jewellery workshops who give them a small commission on whatever is bought.'

'Cham wasn't touting. He thought I might have lost my bearings and offered to walk me back to the hotel. On the way we stopped for a cold drink, and that's when he gave me a language lesson which was so interesting that I forgot the time.'

'He may think you're here for several days and believe in taking his time to get to the object of the exercise. You can bet your life there is one,' was Leonora's cynical reply.

Tonight she was wearing the pleated evening skirt with a vivid green sequinned top. Convinced that Cham's friendliness had had no ulterior motive, but not wishing to argue with her, Angel said politely, 'What a lovely colour your top is.'

'Thank you.' Leonora's response was mechanical and she didn't reciprocate with a favourable remark on Angel's appearance. If it hadn't been for the comment of the woman in the corridor, Angel would have begun to feel that instead of improving her looks she had only succeeded in making a guy of herself.

However, when they went to the restaurant, she sensed from the way other people looked at her that, even if Charles and Leonora were unimpressed, she did look better tonight.

It was after they had decided what to eat and Charles had chosen the wine that he said, 'You have a new watch, I see.'

'Yes, I realised last night that my everyday watch looks wrong with this dress. This watch I bought today was very cheap from a stall in the street.'

'It's a copy of an expensive Cartier watch,' he told her. 'If this were London, I doubt if anyone would guess it wasn't the real thing. A jeweller would know as soon as he opened it, of course. It will be interesting to see how well the gold-plating wears.'

'I thought you disapproved of buying pirated things, Charles,' said Leonora. 'You wouldn't let me buy those cassettes I wanted last time we were here.'

'You knew they were pirated by the price being asked for them. Angel chose this watch because it appealed to her, not because she recognised it as a clever copy of one of the current status symbols. By the way, you said you had two good ideas for what to do when you get to England, Angel. What are they?'

'Oh, yes—well, the first thing I want to do is to get my yachtmaster's certificate, which shouldn't be difficult. And then I thought I'd take a course in cooking. I can do all the basic stuff, but I'd like to know how to make some of the fancy dishes they serve in places like this.'

'With what object?'

'Better catering if I go in for chartering seriously. Your guests will want good food, won't they? Even if you take them ashore to eat a lot of the time, they'll still need some meals on board, and they might as well be good ones.'

'I agree, and I think those are both very sensible suggestions,' said Charles. 'Do you know how to go about getting your yachtmaster's certificate? Did your grandfather have one?'

'He got his years ago, before his first long voyage. I think I may have to wait for my eighteenth birthday to get mine—I'm not sure about that.'

'You could pass for nineteen tonight,' he said, with a smile. 'Where did you have your hair done? In the salon downstairs?'

'Oh, no, I did it myself.'

'Really? Turn your head a moment. Let me see the back.'

Angel obeyed.

'It looks most professional to me. Don't you think so, Leo?'

'Yes, it does,' Leonora agreed. 'But I expect Angel has put it up before. Girls of her age spend hours experimenting with hair and make-up. I did myself in my teens.' She smiled across the table. 'Living alone with your grandfather, inevitably you've missed a lot of the fun that's normal and right for your age group—pop music, discos, discussing Life with your peers, first dates. Never mind, you'll be able to catch up when you get to England.'

Angel was about to reply that she had heard plenty of pop on other people's radios and it didn't appeal to her as much as the classical music she had grown up with, but Charles spoke first.

'I think Angel has bypassed that stage of life. Not everyone goes through it. At eighteen I didn't spend my evenings at discos. I was studying.'

'You were exceptionally clever and serious-minded. You can't compare yourself with ordinary people. I'm sure, if she's truthful, Angel will admit that she would have liked to come nightclubbing with us last night—or, better still, gone to a disco with the young man who chatted her up this afternoon. I know more about teenage girls than you do, Charles. I've been one.' Another smile with a hint of conspiracy in it flashed across the table at Angel. 'All this extra glamour tonight—the hairdo, the earrings, the blue mascara—are for Cham's benefit, not ours. And perhaps also for the handsome young Swiss at Reception.'

Angel had noticed that there was a tall fair-haired man among the Thais who staffed the desk in the lobby. It would have been impossible not to. But the idea that she had put up her hair to impress him or Cham was so far-fetched that it took her breath away. She had put it up for Charles. As the truth of the matter struck her—a truth she had not been aware of until this moment—a rush of warmth flooded her face.

'There, you see, she's blushing,' said Leonora. 'I've only noticed the Swiss boy, but I expect the hotel is full of attractive young men who would like to make a date with Angel if only she were here longer. Never mind, when we get to London I'll make a point of introducing you to Maggie, Angel. She's a junior girl in my office who really has a ball in her spare time. Once you're in her set you won't have a minute to spare—or a dull one!'

Angel climbed into bed and turned out the lights. But she didn't lie down. She sat with her knees pulled up and her arms clasped round them, looking out at the moonlit river flowing endlessly seawards, reminding her of the untroubled life she had led before her grandfather's brief illness.

If it had happened a day earlier or a day later, they would have been somewhere else when he died and she wouldn't be here now. Her life would be going in a different direction towards a completely different future. She wouldn't know that a man called Charles Thetford existed.

Instead of which she was sitting up in bed, watching the flow of the Chao Phraya and facing the fact that she had fallen headlong in love with a man who was forever out of reach. He was older. He was a financial genius. He had a jealous mistress.

Why Leonora should be jealous of someone who had no hope of stealing Charles from her was a puzzle. Perhaps she had foreseen that Angel would fall for him and that alone was enough to make her hostile. Tonight, at dinner, she had done her best to make Angel look gauche, and she had succeeded.

The next night was spent flying to London, leaving Bangkok at one minute to midnight on a non-stop flight to Heathrow which would land at five minutes past six the following morning, local time, after twelve hours in the air.

Leonora had taken a sleeping pill, and as soon as the plane was airborne she put plugs in her ears, covered her eyes with a black silk mask and settled down under a soft vicuña blanket, having instructed the stewardess that she wasn't to be disturbed until breakfast was served.

She had had dinner at the hotel, but Charles preferred to dine in flight, and while Leonora was having a normal dinner he and Angel had eaten only a small omelette and a side salad to stave off hunger until their Thai Airways dinner was served between midnight and one.

As on the flight from Bali, Angel had a free seat beside her, and to give Leonora as little disturbance as possible, Charles came and sat next to Angel for dinner and stayed beside her to watch the movie.

She must have fallen asleep before it was over. When she woke she was covered by a blanket and Charles had gone back to the other side of the aisle and was reading by a thin beam of light from above his head. All the main lights had been turned off, leaving just enough illumination for people to find their way to the heads if necessary.

Angel turned on her side and watched him, thinking that he looked a lot like photographs of Ludo as a young man when his hair had been black instead of white, and his skin still taut over high cheekbones and a strongly-marked jawline.

Ludo had been twenty-nine when he met Eva at a ball during her first season as a débutante. He had married her the following year, soon after her nineteenth birthday. In spite of the difference in their ages, they had been perfect for each other. Wasn't it possible that by the time she was nineteen she, Angel, could have made herself into someone worthy of Charles? Leonora wasn't right for him. There was a core of hardness in her. Relaxed in sleep, her mouth had a petulant droop. And how could Charles like being caressed by those too-long, too-pointed nails? Talons, Ludo would have called them.

Charles turned his head and caught her watching him. He leaned out of his seat, his long body enabling him to speak to her without disturbing those around them.

'Can't you sleep? Would you like a glass of water?'

She shook her head. 'No, thank you.'

He smiled at her, the warm smile which transformed his face and made her insides turn over.

'You're not worrying about things, are you? There's no need to, I promise you.'

The next time she woke he was sleeping, his arms folded across his chest, his head leaning sideways.

In sleep his mouth didn't take on an unpleasant line. Angel found herself wondering what it would be like to be kissed by that mouth. She had no direct experience of kissing, knowing only what she had read about it.

Putting aside the soft blanket which Charles or the stewardess had tucked round her last night, she found her wet pack and went quietly to the washroom.

Her watch, still on Bangkok time, showed it was a few minutes to six. They were about halfway there, somewhere over the Middle East. How amazing really, to be brushing one's teeth in mid-air! The others took it for granted, but to her it was a miracle that all these people and all their baggage could be transported in the space of a night over mountains and deserts and oceans from one side of the world to the other.

As she returned to the cabin, a man rose from his seat and then waited to let her pass. He looked tired and in need of a shave.

'I wish I looked like you after four hours' sleep, young lady,' he said, as she smiled at him.

Ten minutes later Charles woke, flexed his shoulders and arms, ran a hand over his stubble-shadowed jaw and stood up.

'Good morning,' he mouthed at Angel, before disappearing in the direction she had come from.

He came back ten minutes later, his chin with its slight centre dent now smooth again, his hair brushed and the shirt he had slept in replaced with a clean one.

'I'll sit by you, if you don't mind? They won't serve breakfast till eight. Would you like some fruit juice or coffee?' He pressed the bell to summon a steward or stewardess.

Had they been flying in the opposite direction, it would have been daybreak by now with a beautiful eastern dawn to watch as they drank their coffee. Because they were travelling west, the sky outside was still dark when the breakfast menus were brought round and a stewardess gently roused Leonora.

To Angel's surprise she didn't speak to Charles nor he to her before she went to the washroom. They said good morning when she reappeared, freshly made up and bringing with her an aura of some heavy scent which wasn't as pleasant to Angel's nostrils as the light spicy lotion he used.

A low cloud base prevented her seeing the lights of Greater London as they came in to land at Heathrow. A taxi took them to the centre of the city. It was raining, and the wet lamplit streets seemed strangely deserted compared with the bustle of Bangkok.

'We must be mad to live here,' said Leonora morosely, looking out at the early workers scurrying along with hunched shoulders and umbrellas. 'And no doubt I shall find a stack of problems on my desk when I get to the office.'

Angel had heard Charles give two addresses to the driver, the first being Leonora's flat and the second his aunt's house. She was beginning to feel apprehensive that his aunt might not like having an unknown girl foisted on to her.

When the taxi stopped for the first time, Charles sprang out, carrying Leonora's flight bag and offering a hand to help her alight.

Her farewell to Angel was a casual, 'Goodbye', offhand to the point of rudeness.

While the taxi driver unloaded the bulk of the luggage and dumped it on the step of the house to be carried inside by Charles, Angel huddled in her corner of the back seat, inclined to agree with Leonora that anyone who had a choice must be mad to live in this land of cold, dark, wet winter mornings.

She wasn't physically cold because the taxi was heated and before they left the airport Charles had made her put on a sweater he had obviously intended to wear himself, a sweater made of wool even softer than the vicuña blanket. It was nervousness which made her shiver as she waited for him to rejoin her. She wished he was taking her to his house. Already, after less than a week in his company, she dreaded being separated from him. What if his aunt turned out to be like Leonora and took an instant dislike to her?

CHAPTER SIX

'CHARLES, my dear boy! It's always a pleasure to see you—even at half-past seven on a fiendish morning.'

As the woman who had opened the door greeted her nephew, Angel's first thought about her was that she could have been Ludo's sister.

Tall, thin, white-haired and weatherbeaten, she was wearing jeans and a navy blue seaman's sweater over a mannish check shirt. But her bony wrists jingled with feminine silver bracelets as she lifted her arms to hug Charles and kiss him on both cheeks, and a long deep pink Indian silk scarf was wound round her neck with a sparkling brooch pinned to the knot of the bow in which it was tied at the front.

'And this is your protégée,' she said, turning to smile at Angel.

'Evangeline, shortened to Angel,' said Charles. 'Angel, this is my Aunt Dorothea...Miss Thetford.'

'Never mind the Miss Thetford. Call me Dorothea, dear child. Oh, how young you are— and how beautiful!' Instead of shaking hands, his aunt stroked Angel's cheek with a gentle fingertip. 'You'll never believe it, but once I had cheeks like yours. Peaches long since turned to prunes. Never mind, it's not so bad being ancient if one has one's health and a consuming passion to keep one lively. Come inside out of the cold.'

She ushered them inside and led the way down a long hall to the back of the house.

'This is my kitchen-cum-living-room-cum-studio-cum-garden-room . . . the heart of the house,' she explained to Angel, as they entered a large room with glass doors giving on to a spacious conservatory beyond which was a long walled garden. 'Has Charles told you that I'm a sculptor—or, as some people would say, a sculptress, but I prefer the masculine form? Not that I'm a strong feminist, I just like the name sculptor better.'

'I don't think the more recent outbursts of radical feminism have impinged on Angel. She's been somewhat removed from the world as we know it,' said Charles. 'Ah, I see you've waited breakfast for us. We had it on the plane, of course, but a couple of hours before we landed, so we're ready for a second sitting.'

'Home-made muesli and kippers this morning,' said Miss Thetford. 'Show Angel where she can wash her hands, would you, Charles? I'll take her upstairs later on.'

The house had a ground-floor cloakroom and lavatory under the curve of the staircase. The walls of the latter were hung with a great many drawings of small children and cats, and there was one sketch of a skinny long-legged boy with a rabbit in his arms which Angel thought must be Charles aged about nine. His nose was still snub, his cheeks rounded. There was little sign of the authoritative man who had taken charge of her life. Who had been in charge of his life then? So far there had been no mention of his parents. Perhaps, like hers, they had died a long time ago and he rarely thought of them.

To someone raised on a boat where possessions were necessarily few, Miss Thetford's all-purpose room contained an amazing assortment of paraphernalia. Almost every inch of wall had something hanging on it, and every horizontal surface was similarly cluttered. Angel had never seen so many beautiful and interesting things in one place. Even the things on the breakfast table seemed to her unusually pleasing.

'What lovely cups,' she said, lifting a large red-rimmed cup of milky coffee to her lips.

'I bought them in France,' said Miss Thetford. 'The French make the world's best breakfast cups, and this tablecloth comes from a shop in Arles in the south. As you see, I'm a magpie...a compulsive collector. My house is full of souvenirs of my travels; but I never buy things made for the souvenir trade. Those are invariably hideous, as I dare say you've noticed. I can't abide knick-knacks.'

Angel had heard kippers extolled by Ludo, but had never tasted one before because, according to him, a kipper out of a tin was an abomination not to be compared with the genuine article straight from the smoke-house.

The kippers grilled by Miss Thetford, and served on hexagonal plates of deep green earthenware, a perfect foil for the coppery colour of the fish, were indeed delicious. But they made Angel think of her grandfather and of *Sea Fever*, now so far away.

After breakfast Charles called another taxi.

'Shall we see you tonight?' asked his aunt.

He shook his head. 'No, but I'll try to look in tomorrow.'

After he had gone, Miss Thetford showed Angel the room she was to occupy. It was at the top of the house and there was a large black cat asleep on the bed.

'This is Jacob. Turn him out if you don't like cats. There are plenty of other places for him to snooze.'

'Oh, but I do,' said Angel. 'Miss Thetford, it's terribly kind of you to take me in like this. I'm not at all happy about imposing on you.'

'My dear, it's no imposition. I'm delighted to have you. I don't see enough of young people. Being unmarried, I'm in danger of mixing only with my own generation. When Charles was at university and living with me in the vacations, I used to enjoy entertaining his friends.'

'Why did he live with you?'

'He has never got on with his stepmother whom he suspected, I think with justification, of marrying his father for money. Charles's mother died when he was born. Two years later my younger brother, who is dead now, married again, but Sylvia couldn't have children and she wasn't interested in her predecessor's child. Charles was looked after by a nanny and sent away to school at the earliest possible age. Many of his holidays were spent with me. I should have liked to have children, but unfortunately the man I was engaged to marry was killed in the Korean War in the early fifties. A woman with a strong métier has to be madly in love to give up her independence. I only felt that way once. So Charles has been more like a son to me than a nephew.'

'But he doesn't live here any more?' said Angel, who was curious to know where he did live.

'No, no, he hasn't for years. He has a flat in the Barbican which is close to the bank where he works. We don't see a lot of each other. We're both busy people. I suppose we meet about once a month. Either he comes to one of my parties—I enjoy entertaining—or he asks me out to dinner. He takes care of my financial affairs. When I was young, I hardly made enough to live on. Lately I've become rather fashionable and can charge extremely large fees for busts of important men—I've got a Cabinet Minister coming to sit for me this morning. As you haven't had a proper night's rest, why don't you hop into bed for a couple of hours—read if you find you can't sleep—and this afternoon we'll see about kitting you out with some cold weather clothes?'

It seemed strange to go to bed at nine o'clock in the morning, after two lots of breakfast, but Angel felt that she ought to do as her hostess suggested. Once she had settled under the bag of down which took the place of blankets, and Jacob had rearranged himself and was curled against her on the outside of the quilt, she found she was sleepier than she had realised. She closed her eyes, listening to the cat's rhythmic purring, and wondering if Charles had slept here when he was an undergraduate.

On the morning of her eighteenth birthday, Angel was woken by the familiar sensation of Jacob's paws kneading her stomach. She opened her eyes and for a moment they stared at each other before he blinked and looked away. If he found her lying on her back when he came to her room after his nocturnal prowls, he always jumped on to the bed and stepped lightly on to her tummy.

Previously a cat who held aloof from humans but who had lodged with Miss Thetford since turning up as a kitten, from the day of Angel's arrival Jacob had adopted her as the person around whose ankles he would sometimes twine himself and on whose lap he would sit when in a lap-sitting mood.

'Tonight we're having a party, Jacob,' she told him. 'You'll have to stay out of the way or people will stroke you and pet you, and you don't like that, do you?'

As she spoke, she rubbed under his chin, making him purr. From the caresses of strangers he would walk away, but hers he would usually accept. No one, not even she, could pick him up. He would squirm free and scamper off.

'That cat is like a man who's terrified of marriage,' Dorothea had once remarked. 'The merest hint of possessiveness and he's off like a flash.'

Angel loved the black tom, but she didn't intend to let him know it. No sooner had he folded his paws and settled down than she said, 'I'm sorry, dear boy,' and tilted her pelvis, tipping him off her body.

Jacob opened his green eyes wide in a look of pained surprise, but quickly made himself comfortable on the warm place where she had been lying.

Laughing, Angel went to the bathroom. Today, at last, she was a grown-up person with all sorts of rights she hadn't had yesterday. And tonight, for the first time in three weeks, she would be seeing Charles and wearing her beautiful new outfit.

He was the first to arrive. She heard the doorbell ring as she was stepping into her shoes.

He had said he would come early. Angel hurried on to the landing to catch a glimpse of him before he saw her. Leaning over the banisters, she watched Dorothea passing the curl of polished mahogany in which the banister rail ended three floors below. A few moments later she heard them greeting each other. The timbre of Charles's voice sent a little shiver through her.

'Come and have a quiet drink before the others arrive. Angel isn't down yet.'

Dorothea came into view again, wearing a skirt made from an Indian sari with a border of glittering threads and a plain dark silk shirt which she had adorned with Turkish and African beads.

Then Charles appeared close behind her, his hair as thick and glossy as Jacob's fur, and as inviting to the touch. Knowing that she shouldn't be having these thoughts about him when he belonged to someone else, Angel wondered where Leonora was.

Held up at her office and coming later, perhaps. How much nicer the party would be if she weren't coming at all! Dorothea didn't like her either. She had never said so, but Angel could tell. His aunt was perfectly polite to Leonora whenever Charles brought her to the house, but Angel had never seen her touch her, and Miss Thetford was a person who welcomed most regular visitors if not with a hug then with both hands.

Angel went back to her bedroom to take a final look at herself in the full-length mirror. She hoped Charles wouldn't be offended that she wasn't wearing his pearls, but they didn't go with her look for tonight. Because clothes in England were very expensive compared with prices in Indonesia and its neighbouring countries, she had had the idea of trying to make what she wanted. Dorothea owned one of the early electric sewing machines, a heavy black and gold Singer with a polished wooden cover. Although it wouldn't do any fancy stitches, it was ideal for Angel's first attempts at dressmaking.

Tonight's outfit had been inspired by a fashion photograph in *Harpers & Queen*, an expensive magazine which Dorothea didn't buy regularly but of which she had this one issue because it contained photographs of the private view of her most recent exhibition.

The short—very short!—evening skirt which had caught Angel's eye as she looked through the rest of the magazine had been made in the workrooms of an Italian designer and cost nearly a thousand pounds.

The skirt she had made for the party had cost the price of a *Vogue* paper pattern and a reel of silk thread to match the material, which had started life as an evening jacket worn by Charles's grandmother in the Thirties. Dorothea had kept it after her mother died because it was made of beautiful damson and gold brocade. Having worn it herself several times, she had offered it to Angel for her party skirt.

With the skirt, which had a wide tight waistband and pleats to mid-thigh, she was wearing a black leotard, black tights and a pair of inexpensive black suede shoes, with low Louis heels, to which she had added bows made from the damson brocade with an iron-on stiffener. The leotard had a scooped-out neckline which had called for some sort of filling, but not Charles's pearls. In the end, inspired by a portrait of an eighteenth-century French beauty in a low-cut dress with a frilled silk choker, Angel had made a double frill of black lace attached to a black velvet ribbon which tied in a bow at the back.

With her hair, washed that afternoon, piled on top of her head, she felt she had achieved the effect she wanted—young, *à la mode*, and subtly sexy. But whether Charles would approve remained to be seen.

Her heart beating faster than usual, she ran down the stairs to find out.

He and his aunt were in the conservatory. With the chairs removed and the plants grouped more closely together, it provided enough space for dancing to taped music and tonight looked especially pretty with the roof lit by strings of tiny green lights like fireflies.

'Ah, here she is. You look delightful, Angel,' said Dorothea, as she joined them.

Did Charles agree? It was hard to tell. His enigmatic grey gaze took in the frill, the long-sleeved, low-necked leotard, the short skirt, the sheer black tights. But he made no comment, saying only, 'Many happy returns of the day.'

'Thank you.'

He took from his inside pocket an envelope and handed it to her. On it was written, 'To Angel from Charles. Happy birthday.'

She had wondered if he would give her another present and had thought that he probably would. But what could this be? A cheque? A book token?

It turned out to be a voucher for a course of driving lessons. She looked up at him, her eyes shining with pleasure.

'How kind and generous you are!'

Impulsively she reached up to kiss him and Charles inclined his tall head to receive the quick brush of her lips on his lean cheek.

'Everyone should know how to drive. How are your cookery classes going?'

'You'll find that out later. She's prepared tonight's buffet almost single-handed,' said his aunt. 'And she made that very fetching skirt. She's a clever girl who seems to be able to turn her hand to anything. Give her some bubbly, Charles.'

At this point the doorbell rang and Dorothea went to answer it.

'We thought of starting the buffet at half past eight. What time will Leonora be here?' asked Angel, as he handed her a glass of champagne.

'She won't be coming,' he answered. 'Leonora and I have stopped seeing each other.'

'Oh . . . oh, dear. I'm sorry.'

'Are you?' His tone was dry. 'I was under the impression you didn't like her.'

'But you did. It can't be nice when a long . . . friendship comes to an end.'

She wondered what had happened to end it and whose decision it had been. Not Leonora's, she felt sure.

He shrugged. 'These things happen. It was never——' He broke off as his aunt reappeared with the first of the forty people on the guest list.

From then on Angel was kept busy welcoming her fellow students from the catering course and being introduced to the people Miss Thetford had invited, some of them her contemporaries but also several young married couples and a sprinkling of even younger single people. As they had been told it was an eighteenth birthday party for someone from overseas, they had all brought presents, mainly book and cassette tokens and toiletries but including a magnifying make-up mirror, a ring-stand in the form of a china hand, and a clipboard with a matching notebook.

The only thing which stopped the party from being perfect was that Charles didn't dance. But it was a small disappointment compared with her secret delight that his affair with Leonora had come to an end.

About half-past ten he caused a lull in the conversation by tapping a fork against his glass and, when he had everyone's attention, saying, 'Ladies and gentlemen, shall we drink a toast to the girl whose birthday we're celebrating? Some of you have met Angel for the first time tonight, but those of us who have known her longer feel that she's a rather special person, partly because of her unusual upbringing but also because of certain innate qualities. I know you will want to join me in wishing her a long and happy life.'

He looked across the room to where she was standing and raised his glass. 'To Angel . . . may all your dreams come true.'

If only he knew what her most important dream was! she thought, as they drank to her.

Clearing her throat, she said shyly, 'Thank you very much...everyone. And thank you also for your presents. All the birthdays I can remember have been happy days, but I've never had so many presents or a large party before. I'd like to say a special thank you to Dorothea for taking me into her house and making me so welcome and comfortable, and to Charles for bringing me to England. They've both been incredibly kind, and if all my dreams do come true it will be largely due to them for helping me.' She raised her own glass which at the moment contained bitter lemon. 'To Dorothea and Charles—my two kind benefactors.'

She smiled first at Miss Thetford and then at her nephew, wondering if it were possible that, one day, he would make that most important dream come true by returning her love for him.

'That was a charming little speech you made in reply to Charles's toast,' said Dorothea, some hours later when the last guests, including Charles, had gone home and the two of them were drinking hot chocolate as a nightcap. 'Was it entirely impromptu, or had you rehearsed it?'

Angel shook her head. 'I didn't know he was going to propose a toast. He's told you about Leonora?'

'Yes, and I can't say I'm sorry their liaison has come to an end. I've always suspected that her chief interest in Charles was the same as Sylvia's in his father. Sylvia wasn't a career-woman, but just because a woman has achieved success on her own, it doesn't mean she wouldn't rather have a man to pick up the bills. I may be doing her an injustice, but I've always felt that Leonora was a taker rather than a giver, and what Charles needs is someone who will love him for himself, not for the luxurious life he can provide. All the clearing up can wait till the morning. Off you go to your bed, dear child. I must stop calling you that now you're eighteen, mustn't I?'

'I like it,' said Angel. 'I should like you calling me "dear child" if I were twenty-five.'

'It's a pity——' Miss Thetford stopped short and left the remark unfinished. 'I shall set my alarm for an hour later in the morning. I'm getting too old to burn the candle at both ends.'

What had she intended to say? Angel wondered, as she undressed. *It's a pity you're not*: could that have been the thought she had chosen not to express? Was it possible Dorothea guessed how she felt about Charles?

Without Leonora in his life, Charles came to see them more often than he had before. Several times, as the spring advanced, he drove them into the country for lunch on Sunday.

He also took them to the theatre where, during the intervals, Angel saw girls and women eyeing him with interest. She felt it could only be a matter of time before Leonora's successor crossed his path.

From what she had read, and the range of her reading had widened since coming to London, a man accustomed to having a regular partner wouldn't find it easy to give up sex and since Charles, she felt sure, was too fastidious to engage in casual relations, sooner or later he would find another semi-permanent girlfriend.

Or he might even fall in love. The thought terrified her. She was more or less resigned to the fact that she was too young to attract him at present. In a way it might have been better if his relationship with Leonora had continued as a stopgap until Angel had learned enough about life and men to arouse and hold his interest.

Late one afternoon towards the end of April, when they were due to meet him at seven at a concert hall, Dorothea announced that she wasn't feeling up to going.

'I've a pain in my back,' she explained. 'I think I strained it this morning when I was heaving pots around in the garden. It's a pity, but I know I shan't enjoy a concert tonight. I'd rather go to bed early.'

Angel was torn between concern for Dorothea and delight at the prospect of an evening *à deux* with Charles.

'Why don't you go to bed now...at once,' she suggested. It was five o'clock. 'I'll run up and put your electric blanket on for you——warmth is good for bad backs. And then I'll make you a nice supper on a tray so that you don't have to come downstairs again.'

'That sounds lovely,' said Dorothea. 'I expect by tomorrow I'll be as right as rain.'

Angel made a pan of soup, some to keep for tomorrow and some to put in a vacuum flask. Then she cooked a small Spanish omelette which would be good cold with a mixed salad. Finally she arranged a tray which she would carry upstairs before she left the house.

She arrived at the concert hall in good time. When Charles joined her, she explained what had happened.

'We rang your office in case there was someone else who could have had Dorothea's seat, but your secretary said she didn't think you'd wish to be disturbed.'

'No, I was in an important meeting which I particularly didn't want interrupted. She gave me your message later, but I couldn't think of anyone I could ask to join us at such short notice. Poor Aunt D., is she in a great deal of pain?'

'More than she's let on, I expect, but she insisted on my coming without her.'

'Quite rightly. She also insisted on your coming by taxi, I hope.'

He had told her when they first came to London that he would prefer her to travel by bus rather than Underground, and that she was never in any circumstances to use the Tube late at night. But a quarter to seven wasn't late at night, and when she failed to get a taxi after five or six minutes of trying, there had seemed no harm in using the Tube for a short journey at an hour when it would be full of other people going out for the evening.

'No, I came by Tube,' she admitted.

To her dismay, Charles was furious.

'You know my feelings about that. I don't want you exposed to the kind of unpleasant incidents which could happen to a girl of your age on her own!'

'Oh, Charles, that's silly,' she protested. 'Of course I wouldn't use it late at night, but what could possibly happen at this time of the evening?'

'Anything could happen,' he said curtly. 'I'm not keen on your using the Underground at any time of day, but certainly not outside office hours. It's neither advisable nor necessary. Some people have to travel by Tube—you don't.'

'I had no choice. I couldn't get a taxi. About twenty passed me . . . all full.'

'You should have telephoned for one to pick you up from the house. I'm seriously annoyed with you,' he told her sternly.

A heated retort sprang to her lips, but she bit it back, not wanting to make matters worse. What had promised to be a specially enjoyable evening was in danger of going awry. Perhaps if she accepted his censure meekly, his anger would pass off.

After leaving their coats in the cloakrooms, they entered the auditorium and were shown to their seats.

Angel was reading the notes in the programme Charles had bought for her when someone in the row behind touched her on the shoulder. She looked round and saw a vaguely familiar face looking enquiringly down at her from the higher level seats in that row.

'Is your name Angel Dorset?' the fair-haired man asked.

TAKE 4 MEDICAL ROMANCES FREE

Mills & Boon Medical Romances capture the excitement, intrigue and emotion of the busy medical world. A world often interrupted by love and romance...

We will send you 4 Brand New Medical Romances absolutely Free plus a cuddly teddy bear and a surprise mystery gift, as your introduction to this superb series.

At the same time we'll reserve a subscription for you to our Reader Service. Every two months you could receive the 6 latest Medical Romances delivered direct to your door Post and Packing Free, plus a free Newsletter packed with competitions, author news and much, much more.

What's more there's no obligation, you can cancel or suspend your subscription at any time. So you've nothing to lose and a whole world of romance to gain!

Your Free Gifts!

We'll send you this cute little tan and white teddy bear plus a surprise mystery gift when you return this card. So don't delay.

Fill in the Free Books Coupon overleaf ▶▶

Free Books Certificate

Yes! Please send me my 4 Free Medical Romances, together with my Free Teddy and Mystery gift. Please also reserve a special Reader Service subscription for me. If I decide to subscribe, I shall receive 6 superb new books every two months for just £8.10, post and packaging free. If I decide not to subscribe, I shall write you within 10 days. The free books and gifts will be mine to keep in any case.

I understand that I am under no obligation whatsoever - I can cancel or suspend my subscription at any time simply by writing to you.

I am over 18 years of age.

Extra Bonus

We all love surprises, so as well as the Free books and Teddy, here's an intriguing mystery gift especially for you. No clues - send off today!

Mrs/Miss/Ms
(BLOCK CAPITALS PLEASE)

Address _____

_____

Postcode _____ 5AOD

Signature _____

MPS MAILING PREFERENCE SERVICE

Reader Service
FREEPOST
PO Box 236
Croydon
Surrey
CR9 9EL

NO STAMP NEEDED

Send No Money Now

'Yes, it is,' she agreed. Then Charles's wrath, of which she had still been conscious while reading the notes, was driven from her mind as she recognised who had spoken to her.

'Good lord, it's Tim...Tim Bolton!'

CHAPTER SEVEN

'I was fairly sure it was you, but you weren't as pretty at eleven as you are now,' said Tim.

Then he flickered a glance at the man in the seat next to hers, obviously wondering if the compliment had been a gaffe.

Angel laughed and said, 'Thank you,' adding, deliberately, 'And you weren't as handsome. What fun to meet you again, Tim! Do you live in London now?'

'Not all the time. I move around a good deal.'

She thought it was time to introduce him to Charles. But before she could do so, the house lights were dimmed and an expectant hush fell over the audience.

'We'll talk later,' Tim whispered.

She nodded and turned to face forward, stealing a sideways glance at Charles whose expression, in profile, looked extremely forbidding. She was not yet forgiven for disobeying his edict.

Had Miss Thetford been sitting between them, insulating her from the dominant male aura which always emanated from her nephew, Angel would have been able to give her whole attention to the music.

Elbow to elbow with Charles, and with a sailing companion from her childhood sitting immediately behind her, she found it impossible to concentrate on the Bach concerto for two violins being performed on the lighted stage.

Presently another covert glance at Charles showed that his mouth was less tight. The music had calmed and relaxed him. According to his aunt, it had never been ear-blasting decibels of pop music which she had had to ask him to turn down when he stayed with her in his teens. What had, at times, threatened to lift the roof and deafen the neighbours had been the thunderous crescendos of Bach and Beethoven. Classical music had poured through the house like a flood tide, and sometimes Dorothea had gone up to the top floor to deliver a telephone message and found her nephew conducting the symphony which was playing.

'He never wanted to be a musician,' she had told Angel. 'But the movement involved in vigorous conducting was another outlet for his extraordinary energy. He never walked in those days. He took the stairs four at a time—up and down—and he went everywhere at a sprint. He couldn't wait to start conquering the world and, to an extent, he has done that, but I suspect that he isn't really satisfied with his achievements. He wants something more and he hasn't yet found out what it is.'

Perhaps, thought Angel, he blew up about my coming by Tube because his important meeting didn't go as well as he hoped. It was easy to forget that Charles was involved in deals worth millions of pounds, regularly making decisions as vital, in a different way, as the life-and-death decisions of surgeons. She knew that very often the jobs, investments and savings of thousands of people depended on his judgement and he was a man who would be conscious of that, not one who manipulated other people's lives without caring about the effects on them.

When the concerto came to an end and the conductor and soloists took their bows to enthusiastic applause, Angel joined in the clapping, but knew that she might as well have been listening to background music on the radio.

As the lights went up and the applause died down, she said to Charles, 'The man who spoke to me from the row behind us crewed for my grandfather years ago. May I introduce him?'

'By all means.' Charles rose from his seat and turned to appraise Tim, who was also on his feet.

'This is Tim Bolton, who sailed with us when I was eleven,' she said. 'Tim, this is Charles Thetford, who now owns a share of *Sea Fever*.'

The two men said how do you do and shook hands. It was evident that Tim was alone as the people on either side of him were now on their way to the bar.

'Let's go and have a drink,' Charles suggested. 'Do you crew for a living?' he asked Tim, as they moved towards the aisle.

'No, I only sail for fun,' said Tim. 'I'm a photographer by trade.'

'Oh, really? What kind of photographer?'

'I take pictures of interiors for house and garden glossies. If you remember, I was quite keen on photography when your grandfather took me on, Angel. But at that time it didn't occur to me that I might make a career of it. How is Ludo?'

'He died a few months ago...heart trouble.'

'Oh, dear, I'm sorry to hear that. He was a wonderful old guy. I'd have liked to meet him again. Those six weeks I spent with the two of you had a big influence on me—you could say they changed my life. I owe Ludo a lot.'

By this time they had reached the entrance to the bar. Charles said, 'White wine for you, Angel? What can I get for you, Bolton?'

'A gin and tonic, please. Can you manage three drinks? Shall I come with you?'

'No, no, stay and talk to Angel.'

'Is he a relation of yours?' asked Tim, when Charles had left them.

'I met him the night Ludo died when I went ashore for help. Charles has a holiday house in Bali and luckily for me he happened to be there with some guests. Now I'm living with his aunt in London and *Sea Fever* is being completely renovated at his expense. The plan is for him to use her for entertaining for four months a year and the rest of the time I shall charter.'

'I see . . . and what's his line of country? Something very rewarding financially, by the sound of it.'

'He's a consultant with Cornwall Chester. Have you heard of them?'

'The merchant bankers? Who hasn't? They're a big noise in the city. He must be seriously rich.'

'Yes, and seriously kind and nice with it . . . and his aunt is a darling. You must come and meet her. She has the most fascinating house I've ever seen— perhaps she'd let you photograph it.'

Tim laughed. 'I can see you know nothing about my sphere of operations! People queue up to have their houses photographed for the top glossies like *The World of Interiors*, *Architectural Digest*, and *House and Garden*. Some go to amazing lengths to get their places in. It's a status symbol. Others, of course, wouldn't allow us in at any price. They regard it as an invitation to be burgled.'

Charles returned. It was typical of him that instead of juggling with three glasses, he was carrying them on a small tray which he had balanced on one palm as expertly as a waiter.

'You can take this back, if you would?' he said pleasantly to Tim. 'I'll hold your G and T for you.'

'Of course, sir.'

As Tim went to return the tray, Charles pulled down his mouth in a half-amused grimace. 'I don't much care for that "sir". Makes me sound fifty at least!'

'I think it was more in deference to your importance than your age,' said Angel. 'He asked what you did and I told him.'

'How old is he?'

'Twenty-five.'

Her gaze shifted to Tim coming back from the bar. He was not greatly changed from the way she remembered him. Unlike Charles, who was wearing a suit, Tim was in jeans and a sweater, but the jeans were expensive and immaculately clean and the sweater and the shirt underneath it were both of excellent quality. The overall effect was casual but far from scruffy.

'So what are you doing with yourself while you're in London?' he asked her, as he rejoined them.

She explained about the catering course, to be followed by a week studying navigation in Devon before sitting for her yachtmaster's certificate.

'What about you, Tim? You said you were only in London part of the time. Where else are you based?'

'I share a flat with two other guys in Chelsea and I also have a stake in an apartment in New York. It's a slightly crazy set-up; ten of us paying a percentage of the rent of what's called a loft. But a lot of the time I'm on location anyway. Last month I was in the south of Spain, taking pictures of a millionaire's pad at Sotogrande, and next month I'm going to Nantucket, the island off Cape Cod, for a feature on the houses built by whaling captains.'

'It sounds an interesting life,' said Charles.

'Yes, but it has its drawbacks. I can never say where I'll be this time next month, and sometimes not this time next week. There are a lot of freelance photographers competing for the choice assignments. You have to be ready to go when and where you're wanted. It can complicate life,' Tim said wryly. 'Girls don't like having dates cancelled. I'm on my own tonight because the girl who was to have come with me told me to get lost after I had to cancel our last date.'

'How unfair!' said Angel. 'You can't help it if your job means you're more or less permanently on call. The Nantucket assignment sounds fascinating. It's one of my hundred islands. Ludo and I once made a list of a hundred islands we'd like to visit, and Nantucket was one of them. It came between Mustique and Oahu.'

'You must have crossed off at least half the list already, haven't you?' said Tim.

She nodded. 'About that, but none between the Greenwich meridian and longitude ninety west, and that's where a lot of my dream islands lie.'

'Such as?'

'Oh ... Tobago ... Grenada ... the Grenadines ... all the Leewards and Windwards, really.'

'I think you might find the West Indies less romantic than the East Indies,' said Tim. 'I've been to the Caribbean, and the islands with the jet airstrips like Antigua and Barbados have been pretty heavily commercialised in the past few years. They're fine for people from Europe and the northern states of the US who want two weeks in the sun in the middle of winter. But they're not like, for instance, the islands in the south of Thailand which are still undeveloped, or were when you and I and Ludo were there.'

'I agree that parts of the Caribbean have been over-commercialised,' Charles put in. 'But I feel there must still be beaches on the smaller, more remote islands where one can play Robinson Crusoe and look out to sea half expecting to see a galleon on the horizon or a great fleet of turtles passing by. When I was nine or ten, Sir Henry Morgan, who started out as a buccaneer and wound up as governor of Jamaica, was what is called now my role model.'

'Really?' said Angel, surprised. 'I wouldn't have expected you to have those sort of daydreams, Charles, even as a small boy.'

'Other people's daydreams are often surprising,' he said drily. 'Even more so when they're adults.'

Just then the first bell rang. There was only one interval and Tim said, 'In case you want to get away quickly afterwards, may I have your telephone number, Angel? I'd like to keep in touch this time.'

'Of course, but I haven't anything to write it on.'

'I have.' From the back pocket of his jeans, Tim produced a billfold. He took from it a card which he gave to her. 'That's my number, and if Mr Thetford has a pen I can borrow, I'll jot down yours.'

Charles put his hand inside his coat and brought out his tortoiseshell pen. Soon after Tim had returned it to him, the second bell rang and they returned to the auditorium.

Usually, when Charles took his aunt and Angel out, the evening ended with a meal in a restaurant or supper at Miss Thetford's house. Tonight, when the concert was over, they didn't queue for a taxi like many of the other concert-goers. Charles had a car waiting to pick them up.

Having given Miss Thetford's address to the driver, dashing Angel's hope that the evening would end with supper *à deux*, he settled himself on the seat beside her, stretching out his legs which must have been somewhat cramped during the concert.

It was a cool night, and Angel was wearing the long straight navy blue cashmere and wool mixture coat which Miss Thetford had advised her was the classic all-purpose coat for girls of her age to wear as they dashed about London. As she crossed her legs it fell open, revealing her opaque dark tights and the hem of her jersey-knit mini-skirt which tonight she was wearing with a matching lambswool turtleneck and Charles's pearls.

She had dressed to please him, not herself. Since coming to London she had realised that her legs were probably her main attraction from a masculine point of view. But, judging by Leonora's figure, Charles's preference was for other parts of the female anatomy, and although she had filled out a bit lately, Angel felt that her breasts and hips still left much to be desired.

Presently Charles leaned forward and closed the glass partition between them and the driver.

He said, 'I expect Tim will ask you out. Did you ever have a date with a boy while your grandfather was alive?'

'No, I didn't.'

'So I'm right in thinking you're a virgin.'

Angel felt herself starting to blush. 'Yes . . . yes.' The first yes came out too softly and the second too loudly.

'There was a time—before my time—when most girls of eighteen were virgins, but now they're not,' said Charles. 'I read somewhere recently that of eighty-five sixth-form girls questioned about sex, fifty-three per cent had had sex before they were seventeen, twenty per cent thought of sex as "recreational" and only six per cent thought it should be saved for marriage. Whether such questionnaires are reliable is, in my view, debatable. Very few girls in that age group have sufficient strength of character to give answers which might make them seem an oddity. What's your impression of the sex lives of your contemporaries?'

'I don't really know,' said Angel. 'Most of the girls on my course, some of whom are older than I am, have steady boyfriends. Whether they sleep with them or not, I wouldn't know. It's cooking, not sex, we talk about.'

'I imagine so. But if you go out with Tim, sex is something which is bound to crop up. Most young men of his age have the idea that a pass is expected of them. And they don't expect much resistance, if any. So it might be a good idea to sort out your thoughts on the matter.'

'I already have,' said Angel. 'I think people should only make love with people they really care about. I'm not going to jump into bed with anyone unless I love them. So you don't have to worry about me and Tim...if you were worried?' she added questioningly.

'I wouldn't say that,' he answered. 'But I do think your unusual background makes you rather more vulnerable to hurts and disappointments than girls who've grown up in the West. It might be a good idea to make your ideas clear to Tim from the outset.'

'How can I do that?' she asked.

'Don't let him take you back to the flat he shares. Don't ask him to the house when Aunt D.'s not around. Keep things on a friendly basis. You don't have to let him even kiss you goodnight merely because he crewed for your grandfather.'

'I might enjoy it,' she said. 'Even years ago, when nice girls didn't do other things, they'd been kissed at my age. How long am I supposed to wait? It could be years before my true love turns up.'

He made no reply to that, and presently the car drew up outside Miss Thetford's house. Charles sprang out and looked up to her windows on the second floor before helping Angel step out.

'No lights on. She must be asleep.' He leaned down to speak to the driver. 'Wait for me, will you? I won't be more than five minutes.' He straightened and looked down at Angel. 'Give me your key.'

It took her some moments to find it and then he unlocked the front door and reached in to switch on the light. Standing aside for her to precede him into the house, he said, 'I'll come through to the back and check that everything's in order.'

Angel knew that he felt his aunt didn't take enough precautions against break-ins. Miss Thetford's view was that she didn't want to live with her windows barred by security grilles like those of some of her neighbours.

As Charles led the way through to the big room, switching on lights as he went, she said, 'Can't I fix you some supper?'

'No, thanks. I have work to do. There'll be something to eat in my fridge.'

His flat, which she had yet to see, was kept in order by a daily, his refrigerator and food cupboards stocked by the woman who organised the directors' lunches at the bank.

Having satisfied himself that the ground floor was as she had left it, he said, 'Now come and see me out. I'll give Aunt D. a call in the morning.'

On the way back to the front door Angel thanked him for the concert.

'My pleasure,' said Charles.

With his hand on the doorknob, he turned and gave her the thoughtful look she could never fathom.

'Goodnight, Angel. Sleep well.'

To her astonishment, he cupped her face with his free hand and, bending, kissed her on the mouth. The light touch of his lips made her heart lurch wildly in her chest. But it lasted only seconds.

'Something to satisfy your curiosity,' he said.

And then he kissed her again, and this time she felt the excitement shoot deep down inside her.

'Don't forget the bolt and the chain.'

With this down-to-earth admonition, he was gone.

Angel awoke from a vivid dream.

She had been at an orchestral concert, sitting in the front row in a white dress. The man on the rostrum had been Charles, his dark hair dishevelled by the vigour of his head and arm movements. He had been conducting a Rachmaninov concerto with Leonora playing the piano and looking very beautiful in a dress of olive-green satin with a diamond necklace round her throat.

When the music had ended, to thunderous applause, Charles had turned round and bowed, his tanned face glistening with exertion. Then Leonora had come forward to make several curtsies and to receive bouquets of flowers. Finally Charles had kissed her hand and watched her leaving the stage for the last time.

Then he had silenced the continuing applause with a tap of his baton.

'Thank you, ladies and gentlemen. Now I should like to introduce my wife, the former Miss Angel Dorset, to whom I was married this morning and with whom I am about to start my honeymoon. Come up here and take a bow, darling.'

For some moments after waking, Angel remained aglow with the joy she had felt at his announcement. Then, as the reality of the dream faded, she remembered what had happened in the hall and began to ponder whether Charles had kissed her solely for the reason he had given or partly because he had wanted to.

The next evening Tim rang up.

'There wasn't enough time to talk last night. I wondered if you'd like to come out for a meal tonight?'

'I'm sorry, Tim, I'm busy tonight.'

'I knew it was pretty short notice. When do you have a night free?'

'Er...not this week, I'm afraid. When is your trip to Nantucket?'

He gave her the dates.

Angel said, 'Why not ring me when you come back?'

'I'll do that. Keep a night free for me.'

She avoided committing herself. She could have gone out with him tonight, but she had the feeling that it might be better, if Charles said, 'Has Tim called you yet?' to be able to say, 'Yes, and he asked me out, but I said I was busy.'

Then if Charles said 'Why?' she would say, 'Because, although I'd have liked to see the new film at the Leicester Square Odeon, I don't want to start dating someone I'm not really interested in.'

Then Charles might offer to take her to the Odeon himself. And the next time he kissed her goodnight, she wouldn't be too startled to respond.

She would put her arms around his neck and kiss him back.

'Angel? It's Tim—I'm back. When can we get together?'

She had not seen or heard from Charles since the night of the concert, and that was more than three weeks ago. He had spoken to his aunt the following morning and that had been the last time he had been in touch. Perhaps he had met Leonora's successor and was too busy pursuing her to have time to spare for an eighteen year-old virgin.

She said, 'Whenever you like, Tim.'

CHAPTER EIGHT

'MM . . . this is *delicious*!' said Angel, after her first taste of the pizza she and Tim were sharing in a booth of Chelsea's newest pizzeria.

She cut off another chunk with the edge of her fork and put it in her mouth, closing her eyes the better to savour the inspired combination of crispy dough, melted cheese and hot, herby Neapolitan sauce.

A sudden flash of bright light made her give a startled blink.

'I couldn't resist snapping the ecstatic look on your face,' said Tim, grinning and putting down his camera.

He carried it with him at all times. Everywhere he went he took photographs of people, of buildings, of interesting details which Angel, although she was observant, wouldn't have noticed if he hadn't drawn her attention to them.

This was the third time she had been out with him. The first time they had gone to a movie and had a Chinese meal afterwards. The second time they had spent a whole Sunday together, Tim showing her parts of London she would not have discovered by herself, with lunch at a pub and, in the evening, a takeaway curry supper for three at Miss Thetford's house.

Dorothea had liked Tim. 'Very nice manners and a good sense of humour,' had been her opinion of him, reminding Angel that her grandfather had made a similar comment long ago.

'The night we met, at the concert, you said that crewing for Ludo had changed your life. What did you mean?' she asked.

So far they had talked mainly about the present and future and not done much reminiscing about the voyage on *Sea Fever*. Perhaps Tim had hesitated to speak of it in case memories of her grandfather were still unbearably painful to her. At times it did hurt to realise she would never see him again, but in general the happy memories salved the aching sense of loss.

'Up to that point I hadn't been sure that my father wasn't right to be furious with me for slacking at school and not getting the Os and As I needed for a Service commission. But Ludo could see life from both sides. He'd been a worldly success and he'd thrown all that up for a roving life aboard *Sea Fever*. He told me that if he had his life over again, he wouldn't have gone in for law. That was *his* father's influence. When he left school what he secretly wanted to do was to work his passage round the world.'

'If he'd done that, he wouldn't have met my grandmother or, if he had, he would never have got her parents' permission to marry her,' said Angel.

'He'd have met someone else,' said Tim. 'You don't believe there's only one person in the world to be happy with, do you?'

'I'm not sure. Dorothea never met anyone else she wanted to marry after her fiancé was killed.'

'Maybe she saw that it would be better for her, as an artist, not to be bothered with a husband and children. Getting married isn't obligatory—it's a choice people make. That's what Ludo made me see. That life is a matter of choices and you don't have to do what everyone else does or what other people think you should do. You have to sit down and decide what you want for yourself.'

'But people can't always have what they want. It's no use wanting to be a ballet dancer if you're too tall, or a champion skier if you grow up in Fiji.'

'That's right,' Tim agreed. 'The first thing is to distinguish between crazy pipe-dreams and practical possibilities.'

Angel sipped the glass of red wine he had ordered to go with the pizza. For several days after Charles had kissed her goodnight, wanting to spend the rest of her life with him had seemed a practical possibility. Tonight it seemed a crazy pipe-dream.

As Tim walked her home she wondered if, when they got there, he would give her a goodnight kiss. So far he had shown no sign of feeling that a pass was expected of him. She wondered if he might have been seriously fond of the girl who had cut him out of her life and he wasn't ready for another relationship yet. So far his manner towards Angel had been that of an older brother.

'I'll see you on Friday, right?' he said, when they came to her door. And that, with a friendly pat on the shoulder, was how he said goodnight.

Dorothea was making pastry. She did things when the mood took her and quite often started cooking for the freezer late at night. She was not on her own. Charles was sitting at the other end of the kitchen table. He stood up as Angel came into the room. Wasn't it just her luck that he should finally show up on a night when she was out with Tim, she thought vexedly.

'Hello,' he said. 'How are you?'

'Fine, thanks. How are you?'

'I'm just back from Barcelona.'

'Bearing gifts,' said his aunt. 'Look at what he's brought me. Isn't it lovely?'

Her hands being floury, she nodded her head at the bench on which lay a stylish blouson of dark red leather.

'It's gorgeous,' said Angel, feeling the soft, supple texture.

'I chose some trousers for you. I hope they fit,' said Charles. He handed her a shiny carrier bag with the name *Loewe* on it. Inside, folded in tissue, were a pair of greige suede trousers.

'Oh, Charles, they're gorgeous! How kind of you.'

'Go and try them on. If they don't fit, there's a branch of *Loewe* in Bond Street where I'm assured you can change them.'

She ran up to her room and came down a few minutes later wearing the trousers with a cream sweater.

'They fit perfectly. I feel like a million dollars in them. Thank you ... thank you very much.'

'*De nada*, as they say in Spain. I hear you've been out with Tim Bolton. Had a good time?'

'Yes, thank you. What were you doing in Spain, apart from shopping for us?'

'It was a business trip. My travels aren't as interesting as young Bolton's,' Charles said dismissively. 'I must go. Goodnight, Aunt D.' He kissed his aunt on the cheek and gave Angel an un-smiling nod. 'Goodnight.'

'I'll see you out.' As they walked along the hall, the only thing she could think of to say was, 'Don't you want to ring for a taxi?'

'No, I'll pick one up later, but I want to walk part of the way. I haven't had enough exercise recently.'

'Charles looks tired,' said his aunt, when Angel returned to the kitchen. 'I suppose he'll go back to that soulless flat he calls home and work till two in the morning. It's not my idea of a rich full life. He needs a companion, someone to make him relax and do something more rewarding than merely making money for himself and other people.'

'Perhaps he has a companion that we don't know about yet. She may have helped him to choose your jacket and my trousers,' suggested Angel.

'I doubt that. Charles isn't the sort of man who needs a woman to go shopping with him, and if he had found another girlfriend he wouldn't be so ir-ritable.' Dorothea gave her a keen look. 'You weren't very forthcoming about your date with Tim. *Did* you enjoy yourself?'

'We had a terrific pizza.'

But not so terrific that it was worth not being here when Charles came, thought Angel forlornly.

On Thursday Tim rang up to postpone their date because he had been given an unexpected as-signment to photograph a village in southern Italy.

'Never mind,' Angel said philosophically.

The truth was that she was relieved. Much as she enjoyed Tim's company, she would rather sit at home every night for a year than be out the next time Charles called.

She was still waiting for that longed-for eventuality when she ran into Leonora.

It was on a Saturday morning that they came face to face in a street near Miss Thetford's house. It was one of those streets to be found all over London which are much the same as a village high street, with a chemist, a newsagent, a florist and various other small shops. This particular street also had two restaurants, a furrier, a fashionable hairdressing salon and two expensive dress shops, one of which attracted customers from far beyond the immediate neighbourhood.

Angel had been to the paper shop to pay Dorothea's monthly bill when she saw Leonora emerging from the dress shop with a carrier bag and the pleased face of a woman who had just bought something extremely becoming. But that expression changed when she saw who was walking towards her.

'Hello, Leonora,' Angel said politely.

Even though Charles's ex-mistress was looking daggers at her, she felt obliged to stop and exchange a few words.

At first she thought the older woman was going to cut her dead. But then Leonora's mouth formed a patently insincere smile and she said, 'Oh, hello, Angel . . . how are you?'

'Very well, thanks. And you?'

'I'm surviving. You wouldn't expect me to be on top of the world, would you? Not after having my friendship with Charles wrecked by your arrival on the scene.'

'I don't think I had anything to do with the ending of your relationship,' Angel said uncomfortably.

'You don't? I do. I think you had everything to do with it. We weren't about to break up *before* you burst into our lives with your big blue eyes and your helpless look. We'd been together for two years and would be together still if it weren't for you.'

At first Angel didn't know what to say. She didn't believe the accusation was true. How could it be? Whatever had brought an end to Charles's liaison with this woman, it couldn't have been her doing. How could she have wrecked an affair which was sound and strong? Obviously it had been starting to break up some time before that anguished night at Bali.

'I think you're deceiving yourself,' she said quietly.

'And you're deceiving yourself if you think that Charles will ever fall for you,' was Leonora's angry retort. 'I don't suppose you know it yet, but what you are is a guinea-pig. Charles has never found a real woman to match up to his ideal. When you came along he realised he could mould you any way he wanted. That's your attraction, my dear. You're malleable. He can make you fit his blueprint.'

'But I hardly ever see him,' Angel countered.

Leonora looked surprised at that. It took the wind out of her sails for a moment.

Recovering herself, she said, 'I've no doubt you eat out of his hand when you do see him. It was obvious you were dazzled by him from day one. Do you think I didn't know what that attempt to upstage me on our second night at Bangkok was all about? Of course I did. And I'll tell you the reason why it worked. You probably thought you looked amazingly glamorous. Well, you didn't, my dear. You looked like a little girl who's been trying out her mother's cosmetics, and Charles saw that and liked it.'

She looked Angel up and down and then shrugged her shoulders. 'It may be that, having grown up under a man's thumb, you won't mind conforming to the pattern of perfection Charles has in mind. But just make sure that you never step out of line, never answer back, never argue, never want to do your own thing. Because if you do, dear sweet little innocent virgin, you will find yourself dropped the way I was.'

She unzipped her small shoulder bag and rummaged inside it. Angel thought she might be on the verge of tears and looking for a tissue, but it was a small bunch of keys which Leonora had wanted.

'Give my regards to Pygmalion when next you see him,' she said, in a sarcastic tone, before turning away to unlock a car parked at one of the meters.

Dorothea was out when Angel got back to the house. She looked up Pygmalion in the encyclopaedia.

A legendary king of Cyprus who made an ivory statue (known as Galatea in modern versions of the story) and fell in love with it. When he prayed for a wife who would be as beautiful as the statue, Aphrodite (in Greek mythology the goddess of love) gave the statue life and Pygmalion married her.

Angel closed the heavy volume and put it back on the shelf. She didn't know what to think about Leonora's embittered allegations. Was there an element of truth in them? Was Charles attracted to her because of her inexperience? Was he, at heart, an old-fashioned sexist who thought men and women should live by different rules and regretted the days when women had been dependent and subservient?

She was still wondering and worrying about the unpleasant encounter outside the dress shop when Dorothea returned.

'Shortly after you went out, Charles telephoned to ask us to have dinner with him,' said his aunt. 'I told him I was already committed tonight but that you were free. He'll call for you at half-past seven.'

'Did he say where we'd be eating and what I should wear?' Angel asked, trying to sound casual.

'At some new trattoria in Bayswater. Informal, I gathered.'

After lunch they went for an energetic walk in Hyde Park. Later Angel did her nails and washed her hair. She decided to wear the Spanish suede trousers with a soft angora sweater with padded shoulders and pieces of silk appliquéd in an abstract design, embellished with beads, on the front. A wide imitation tortoiseshell bangle and matching hoop earrings were the finishing touches.

Miss Thetford left the house by taxi at a quarter-past seven and Angel spent the next fifteen minutes wondering if tonight she had too little make-up on.

Leonora's jibe about her attempt to look more sophisticated in Bangkok had made her nervous of repeating that mistake—if in fact she had overdone it that night. Maybe there had been more cattiness than truth in the barbed comment.

The doorbell rang while she was staring anxiously at her reflection in the huge looking-glass fixed to one wall in the hall. She hurried to open the door. It was raining slightly; Charles was holding an open umbrella to protect her from the drizzle and there was a taxi with its engine running at the kerb.

'Hello, Charles. I wasn't sure if you'd be coming in for a drink. I shan't be a sec. My bag and mac are right here.'

Her latchkey was already in her pocket, because, like that of many houses in London, the door had two locks. It took only seconds to shrug on her raincoat and join him on the doorstep, closing the door behind her and quickly inserting and turning the key in the lower lock. Moments later she was settling herself in the back of the taxi and her second evening alone with him had begun. Would it end the same way as the first one? she wondered, her pulses fluttering at the memory of his goodnight kisses.

'Why are you smiling?' she asked, an hour later.

'I was comparing your plate with the one on the table opposite,' said Charles.

Angel glanced at the couple dining on the other side of the room. The girl had chosen the same main course as she had and had also finished eating. But judging by what was left on her plate, she could only have swallowed a few mouthfuls. On Angel's all that remained was a neat pile of small empty shells. Every morsel of the spaghetti and sauce which had accompanied them had disappeared.

'I think it's wrong to waste food,' she said, in a lowered voice. 'If she's worried about her weight, why not order a salad? If I were a man, I wouldn't date a girl twice if she chose an expensive dish and left most of it. Would you?'

'I wouldn't myself, but it may be that her host expects a different return on his investment than the pleasure it's given me to watch you eat with relish while his companion merely rearranged her food,' Charles replied drily. 'Have you room for a pudding?'

'Yes, please.' Angel had seen some delicious-looking confections passing by on the pudding trolley. 'But perhaps we could have a little pause first.'

'By all means. I've been thinking over something you said the last time we went out together.'

He paused as the Italian waiter came to remove their plates and replenish their glasses with the wine Charles had ordered. Angel thought back to the night of the concert, wondering what she could have said to interest him to the extent of thinking about it afterwards.

'You would like a sweet?' the waiter enquired.

'Not immediately.' When he had gone, Charles went on, 'You were talking about your list of islands...most of your dream islands being, like mine, in the Caribbean. That being so, I feel it would be a good idea to have *Sea Fever* moved there. What do you think?'

'I think that would be fine, but it's a long way from Bali to the Caribbean and——'

'I wasn't suggesting she should be sailed there. When her refit is completed, she can be transported on the deck of a freighter. It happens all the time. How do you think international ocean racers get about the world? Not under sail.'

'I suppose not, but wouldn't it cost an awful lot of money to have her transported...and where to?'

'I'm advised that English Harbour, Antigua would be an excellent base for her. I brought some details to show you.' Charles unzipped the leather document case which was lying on the banquette beside him. Angel had wondered why he had it with him and assumed he must have collected her straight from the bank.

Later, when they had both had some lemon cheesecake and were finishing the meal with coffee and candied figs, Angel debated mentioning her meeting with Leonora and seeing how Charles reacted, especially if she reported the angry red-head's parting shot. But the evening had gone so well that she didn't want to risk spoiling it.

'When's your next date with Tim Bolton?' Charles enquired suddenly.

'I don't know when I'll be seeing him again, and our meetings aren't really dates in the usual sense. We're just friends who are not the same sex. That is possible, you know.'

'Is it? Not in my experience.'

'Well, I'm sure your experience is extensive, but perhaps that's one you've missed out on.'

'Not the only one.' His grey eyes were sombre as he made this remark.

He was having a liqueur with his coffee and his right wrist was resting on the edge of the table while his long fingers toyed with the stem of the glass. Angel had a strong impulse to lay her hand on his arm and give it an affectionate squeeze. But she didn't.

He switched his gaze from the glass to her face. Quickly she looked away, afraid he would see in her eyes what she felt for him.

'Dorothea is going to miss you when you go back to sea,' he said. 'She told me this morning how much she enjoys having you with her.'

'I love being there. I expect the boat will seem terribly cramped now that I'm used to more space.'

'You aren't tempted to change your life and come ashore permanently?'

'How can I? I have to earn my living, and the sea is the only place where I can do that.'

'Not necessarily. The other girls on your course are going to be catering on land. So could you.'

'But the sea has been my life. I should miss it terribly—unless I had something very special to replace it.' After a slight pause Angel added, 'Or someone very special.'

'What you need,' said Charles, 'is a younger version of your grandfather. Someone who knows the sea as well as he did.'

'Not necessarily. The man in my life will have to be someone with Ludo's personal characteristics— kindness, tolerance, a marvellous sense of humour—but he may not have the same skills. All the world's nicest men aren't sailors,' she said, with a smile.

He didn't respond to her joke. 'The man in your life will come later. You're too young to be thinking of marriage. Just don't let yourself be embroiled in pointless affairs. Stick to your guns and don't go jumping into bed until you know what you feel is for keeps,' he advised her.

'I'm as old as my grandmother when she fell in love with Ludo. She took one look at him and knew she would never look at anyone else, and she didn't. Nor did he.'

'How old were they when they married?'

'She was nineteen. He was thirty.'

'A year older than you. Three years younger than I. It's a big age gap.'

Was he only referring to Eva and Ludo, or also to herself and him? she wondered.

She said, 'I don't think age matters particularly if people are on the same wavelength. I mean, look at the age gap between Ludo and me, but we got on brilliantly.'

'Yes, it sounds as if you did.'

The waiter came to refill their coffee-cups. Afterwards Charles started a new line of conversation by asking her opinion of a controversial issue reported in the morning papers.

It wasn't late when he took her home. No light showed through the fanlight above the front door, which meant that his aunt was still out.

'I'll wait till she gets back,' he said.

'Would you like some more coffee?' asked Angel, unbuttoning her raincoat.

'Yes, as long as it's decaffeinated.' Charles helped her to take it off and then tossed it over the newel post.

'Does strong coffee keep you awake?'

'Among other things.'

He followed her through to the big room where, as she put the lights on, Jacob sat up and stretched, showing the rose-pink roof of his mouth as he opened it wide in a yawn.

''Allo, Monsieur Miaow. 'Ow are you zis evening?' Angel had got into the habit of chatting to him in a stage French accent and spoke to him thus without thinking, realising too late that Charles might consider it silly.

To her surprise, he said, 'You've seen Peter Ustinov playing Hercule Poirot, I take it?'

She shook her head. 'Why do you ask?'

'The cat reminds one of Ustinov in that part. He's a splendid actor and an even better raconteur. I have some tapes of interviews he's given on television. I must play them to you some time—you'll be on the floor.'

'I'll remind you.'

Would Charles also be on the floor with laughter? she wondered. That was something she would like to see.

They had coffee in the conservatory kept, all year round, at a temperature which would allow his aunt to grow plants which wouldn't survive even under glass without some heating.

'Dorothea told me you gave her this room for her sixtieth birthday...something she'd always wanted but felt she couldn't afford,' said Angel. 'That was a nice thing to do.'

He shrugged. 'I could afford it easily and I knew * was something she wanted.'

'But another man might not have thought of it or, having thought of it, done it.'

They were sitting in old Lloyd Loom chairs which had been resprayed a soft green to merge with the greenery around them. Charles replaced his cup and saucer on the cane and glass table between their chairs.

'Don't think too highly of me. My faults are legion,' he said, at his most sardonic.

As she put her cup aside, he rose to his feet and, taking her hands, drew her up to stand in front of him.

'If I were a better man I shouldn't be doing this,' he said, looking down at her.

There was a gleam in his eyes she had seen before, but only in films. The desire she saw in Charles's face was real and a little frightening in its intensity.

She held her breath as he placed her hands against his chest and put his arms round her.

CHAPTER NINE

THIS time his first kiss was like the second kiss last time. After some seconds Angel began to kiss back, her lips instinctively responding to the soft movements of his.

It was rather like dancing, she found. The kind of dancing called 'nightclub shuffle'; not a matter of knowing any steps but going with the flow of the music.

Almost at once she knew that it would be better if her arms were not trapped between them but were round his neck. When she did something about this Charles seemed to think for a moment that she was trying to break free. His hold on her slackened. But when, standing on tiptoe, she locked her arms round his neck and pressed herself lovingly against him, he gave a strange smothered groan and crushed her to him, making her feel the latent strength she had known he had since seeing him swimming off Bali.

To be powerless in a man's arms was a strange sensation which she knew she wouldn't have liked with anyone else. With him it was exciting. Her whole body seemed to be melting as if she were made of wax. But, unlike a candle which had its flame outside it, hers was an internal flame, a fire which flickered and burned along every nerve.

The kiss was going really wild when suddenly he ɔke it off. They had both heard the sound of the front door being opened, but Angel had been too far gone to come down to earth as quickly as he did.

'I expect Angel is in the kitchen, or she may have gone up to bed. No, her raincoat is over the banisters. She must still be downstairs.'

Dazedly aware that Dorothea must have brought someone home with her, Angel watched Charles take the handkerchief from his breast pocket. First he used it to remove lipstick smears from around her mouth. Then, quickly, he rubbed traces of colour from his own. He was breathing more deeply than usual, as if he had just stopped running.

By the time Miss Thetford entered the kitchen, followed by a man Angel had never seen before, Charles's handkerchief was back in his pocket and he was in full control of himself.

'Oh, you're here too, Charles. How nice,' said his aunt, when she saw them in the conservatory.

He had made Angel sit down, pushing her into her chair with gentle force because, as doubtless he could tell, she was still in a daze.

Miss Thetford turned to the grey-haired man who must have offered to run her home from the dinner party.

'Professor, let me introduce Angel Dorset who lives with me, and my nephew, Charles Thetford. This is Professor Kingsland, one of our most distinguished surgeons.'

Angel stood up to shake hands. She wondered if the surgeon could tell that her heart was still racing and her nerves quivering.

While the two men were shaking hands, she said to Dorothea, 'Shall I make some more coffee?'

'Ralph prefers China tea. I'll share a pot with him. Thank you, dear.'

Half an hour later, by which time Angel had calmed down, Charles got up to go. 'Come and see me out, will you?' he said to her.

After he had said goodbye to the surgeon, Angel also said goodnight to the two older people. If Charles meant to kiss her again in the hall, she wanted to be able to recover in private in her bedroom.

But Charles didn't kiss her again. At the door, he said, 'I think it's just as well Lesson Two was brought to that abrupt conclusion. You have a natural aptitude which took us further than I'd intended.'

Taking the tip of her nose between the knuckles of his first two fingers and giving it a little squeeze— a caress she had seen given to small children—he said, 'Goodnight.'

She was awake until three, reliving those heavenly all-too-brief minutes in his arms, longing for Lesson Three.

Was he awake too? Wanting to make love to her? There could no longer be any doubt that he desired her. The way he had kissed her had proved that. But desire and love were not always concomitant. He had wanted Leonora's body but hadn't loved her.

If she hadn't met Leonora, Angel would have lain awake happier than she had ever been in her life. But her memory of the morning's encounter kept ___ng on and spoiling her enjoyment in reliving ___ening. Try as she might, she couldn't rid herself of the uneasy feeling that for Charles to have fallen in love with her was too good to be true. Maybe Leonora was right. Maybe he wasn't in love with her, but with an ideal which he thought he could make her match.

What was his ideal woman like? Perhaps, the next time they met, in a roundabout way she could ask him.

At breakfast the following morning Angel wouldn't have been surprised if Dorothea had made some oblique, gently teasing reference to what had been happening in the conservatory when she and Professor Kingsland had entered the house. Miss Thetford had very sharp eyes which missed nothing. She was quick to pick up every nuance in other people's conversation. Surely she must have felt the vibrations in the garden room?

If she had, she chose to ignore them. In fact she was noticeably withdrawn, saying little about the dinner party and not asking about Angel's evening.

Angel began to wonder if she *had* picked up the vibrations and wasn't pleased. She had disapproved of Charles's relationship with Leonora; she might be strongly opposed to him starting something with someone as young as Angel.

For several days this new and marked reserve continued until Angel felt she could bear it no longer.

One evening, during supper, she said, 'Dorothea . . . are you annoyed with me?'

Miss Thetford looked surprised. 'Of course not dear child. Why should I be annoyed with you'

'You haven't talked to me much for the last few days. I felt I might have displeased you.'

The older woman put down her knife and fork and reached a hand across the table to pat Angel's arm.

'I'm sorry, my dear... have I been as abstracted as that? I didn't realise it was showing. The fact is——' She paused uncertainly. 'You'll think I've gone mad, I expect, but the fact is I've lost my heart to Ralph Kingsland. I can't stop thinking about him... wishing he'd ring me. He said he was going to, but he hasn't. Perhaps it was just one of those things people say without really meaning them.'

Angel was amazed and greatly relieved by this confession.

'I'm sure it wasn't,' she said. 'He wouldn't have brought you home if he hadn't liked you, but he's probably terribly busy. Perhaps several emergency operations have cropped up. Is he a bachelor or a widower?'

'Oh, not a bachelor. I should be *very* wary of a man of his age who had never been married. He's a widower with four grown-up children who are scattered all over the world, so he only sees them occasionally.'

The next day Dorothea got her call from Professor Kingsland and an invitation to go to the theatre with him. Angel got a postcard from Italy.

The picture side of the card showed a *ceramista* at work on a tall earthenware pot with twin handles. n the reverse was the message—'Should be back soon after this reaches you. Interesting trip. Lots to tell. Love, Tim.'

Angel felt sure the 'love' wasn't meant to be taken for more than friendly affection. She wished that, like Dorothea, she had a date with her love. When would she see Charles again? Every day seemed like a year while she waited to hear from him, yet whenever they were together hours seemed to flash past like minutes.

She didn't see him or hear from him until Dorothea gave one of her Sunday lunch parties to which she invited Professor Kingsland and Charles and a couple of artists who were not married but had lived together for twenty years and hyphenated their surnames. Ian and Gina had met while back-packing in the East with companions of their own sex.

'If we'd been on our own, we'd have joined forces straight away, but we couldn't leave our friends in the lurch, so we only had two weeks together before we had to separate. It was the longest six months of my life before I saw Ian again,' said Gina, during lunch.

'Mine too,' said her partner.

Clearly they were still very happy together.

After lunch Charles said to Angel, 'Come for a turn round the garden.'

Leaving the others relaxing in the conservatory, they walked down the long narrow garden which was starting to show signs of spring.

'I'm flying to Japan tomorrow. I'll be away for two weeks, coming back via Canada,' he told her.

'How I wish I could come with you! I'd love to go to Japan.'

'It's an interesting country and in parts very beautiful. My schedule never allows enough time to enjoy it.'

'Can't you make time?'

'Not on this trip.'

'Ludo would have quoted Wordsworth to you. "Getting and spending, we lay waste our powers." Do you know that poem?'

He nodded. 'And I plan to emulate your grandfather and give up "the sordid boon", perhaps rather younger than he did. But not for a few years yet.' He smiled at her. 'Not until I have enough in my piggy-bank to ensure that I and those in my care have the means to keep us in comfort in perpetuity, as the lawyers say.'

'I think your idea of comfort is my idea of luxury,' she said. 'And how do you know that you've got enough years ahead of you to put off the time for enjoying life?'

'Good God! I'm not that old,' he said almost brusquely.

'That's not what I meant. People die or get killed at my age. Who was it wrote "Look thy last on all things lovely every hour"?'

'It was Walter de la Mare, and that's what I'm doing at this moment . . . looking at a lovely face I shan't see again for two weeks.'

Angel caught her breath. His grey eyes held the same glint she had seen in them before he kissed her. Was he going to kiss her again, here in full view of the others?

Charles thrust both hands into the pockets of his ers in a movement which gave the impression

that, if he hadn't, he might have reached out and
pulled her to him. Or was she only imagining it?

'I—I shall miss you,' she said.

'I hope so.'

For a moment longer he looked down into her
eyes and then he began to walk back in the direction
of the house, and shortly afterwards he left, saying
goodbye to her with a handshake as if she meant
no more to him than Gina did.

But although she couldn't be sure he had wanted
to kiss her in the garden, she had one heartening
fact to hug to her during his absence. He had said
she had a lovely face.

'Hi! I'm back and I've got some great news. Tony
Sheringham wants to meet you!'

Tim's voice on the telephone sounded as if he
were announcing that she had won some fantastic
prize in a competition.

'Who's Tony Sheringham?' asked Angel.

'Oh, come on, you must have heard of him. He's
the top fashion photographer. The glossies are full
of his pictures.'

'Why does he want to meet me?' she said,
mystified.

'Because I showed him a folder of pictures I took
of you and he's impressed. He knows potential
when he sees it. Look, can I come round right
away? Tony's still got the folder, but I've got a
duplicate set. When you see them you'll understand. You're seriously photogenic, Angel. You're
one of those lucky people the camera loves.'

Half an hour later he was with her, spreading
dozen large prints on the kitchen table.

'Now...d'you see what I mean...you look great from every angle...even with your mouth full of pizza!'

Angel had forgotten the flash photo he had taken of her in the pizzeria. She did remember being snapped while she was playing with a puppy in the park, but she hadn't known she was having her back view photographed while she was stretched over the top of a wide stone balustrade, upended like a schoolboy awaiting a caning, all mini-skirted bottom and long navy blue legs.

'Tony said that reminded him of a classic shot of Jean Shrimpton, one of the Sixties' top models, in a pair of wool stockings,' said Tim. 'He's a lot older than we are, forty...maybe forty-five. He's been in the business a long time. He remembers when Twiggy got started. He thinks you could be as big a hit as she was.'

'Twiggy? What a funny name.' Angel was still studying the prints.

'She's an actress now. I keep forgetting you haven't heard of people who are household names to everyone else.'

Angel forbore to point out that many names which were famous in Asia were virtually unknown in Europe. She had noticed on the catering course that most of her fellow students knew little or nothing about the part of the world she came from, although some of them wanted to travel and asked her about it. Charles had an international outlook; he was truly a man of the world. But Tim, although he had travelled, was curiously insular in some of his attitudes. Perhaps he had inherited them from father.

'I don't think you've got the message... with Tony behind you, you could go straight to the top, and top models earn big bucks,' he said.

To Angel it sounded as unlikely as winning the football pools or breaking the bank at Monte Carlo, which she knew about from a catchy music-hall song which Ludo had taught her when she was small.

'Why with him behind me?' she asked 'Why not with you behind me? You took these pictures?'

'Yes, but only to get him interested. Fashion's not my line of country, it's a different ball game Tony knows everyone who's anyone on all the fashion glossies. You're to meet him on Wednesday morning. He'll lay on a hair stylist and make-up person, and the pictures he'll take will make these look like amateur night.'

'But I'm busy on Wednesday—you know that.'

'Angel dear, this is your big chance,' said Tim, with exaggerated patience. 'You'll have to make some excuse to skip your classes that morning. This is far more important. A successful model earns more in an hour than most girls earn in a month. In two or three years, with Charles to help you invest the money you'd earn, you could be seriously rich.'

'I don't think Charles would approve. I'm sure he wouldn't.'

'Are you crazy? A banker disapprove of making money? Anyway, it's not up to Charles. It's up to you. Don't you want to be independent? Don't you want to be successful? I knew the minute I saw you it was a possibility, but I didn't want to raise your hopes until I'd got Tony's opinion.'

Seeing she was still unconvinced he said, with a trace of anger, 'Look, if I walked down Oxford Street and asked fifty girls if they'd like to do a test with Tony Sheringham, I'd have all fifty lined up like that.' He snapped his fingers. 'It's the chance of a lifetime!'

Angel didn't want to annoy him when clearly he had gone to a lot of trouble on her behalf. 'All right: I'll be there,' she agreed.

Tim rolled his eyes upwards. 'She'll do it! This blasé young lady will kindly condescend to accept an opportunity which anyone else would kill for,' he said sarcastically. Then his enthusiasm overcame his exasperation and he seized her in a boisterous hug. 'You're going to be a name—I feel it in my bones! You're going to be as big as Marie Helvin was, and Jerry Hall. But they were Eighties names. You're the face of the Nineties.'

There was no sign of Tony Sheringham when Angel arrived at the rented studio where she was to meet him. But the people who were going to prepare her for the photographic session were waiting for her in a changing-room with whitewashed brick walls and a long mirror and counter.

The girl stylist had already plugged in a set of rollers, and the make-up man—who looked decidedly effeminate, Angel thought—was unpacking a case of cosmetics. Evidently they had worked together before and, after saying hello to her and introducing themselves, they continued the conversation they'd been having before she arrived.

First the stylist, Liz, wound Angel's hair on the ~~lers~~, and then she moved away to unpack a box of clothes and hang them on a portable clothes rail while her colleague, Marty, set to work.

Perched on a high stool, Angel watched him apply a basic foundation and then add lighter and darker shades to emphasise the modelling of her features. He did everything quickly and deftly, but there were so many stages that it still took a long time. Although she had naturally long eyelashes, he seemed to consider it necessary to apply extra lashes, one by one, to the outer sides of her eyelids. He also changed and enlarged the shape of her mouth with a brick-coloured pencil before filling in the new outline with lipstick followed by a coat of gloss.

When, at last, he had finished, Liz, who had interrupted Marty's work to take off the rollers some time ago, continued the transformation of Angel's hair from her own straight and simple style into a turbulent cloud of what Dorothea called Gorgon's locks, her name for hairstyles which reminded her of the hissing serpents on the heads of the three mythological sisters, Medusa, Euryale and Stheno.

Angel didn't like the way she looked when they had finished with her, and she knew Dorothea wouldn't approve and Charles would be horrified. He would never have called her face 'lovely' looking as it did now. But Liz and Marty seemed delighted with their handiwork.

Marty had gone to get a coffee and Liz was helping her to put on one of the dresses from the rail when there was a perfunctory tap on the door and a man walked in and looked her up and down

He didn't smile and say hello or tell her who he was. He said, 'As soon as you're ready, we'll st

'That was the great Tony Sheringham, I presume?' Angel said to Liz when he had turned and walked out.

'Yes . . . in one of his grumpy moods, by the look of him. You'd better watch your step,' said the stylist. She gave a finishing tweak to some of the wisps round Angel's ears. 'Right, off you go, love.'

When Angel walked into the studio, one end was ablaze with light and an assistant was rearranging some white paper screens in accordance with Tony's instruction.

Angel walked up to him. 'Good morning. I'm Evangeline Dorset. How do you do?' She held out her hand.

Looking surprised, he took it, and she gave him her firmest clasp which, after years of crewing, had a good deal of more muscle behind it than most girls' handshakes.

'Tim said your name was Angel.'

'That's what my close friends call me. To everyone else I'm Evangeline, Mr. Sheringham. I'm ready when you are.'

Two days before he was due back, Angel posted a letter to Charles at his flat.

After saying she hoped his trip had been successful, and that she realised he would have a lot to do immediately after his return, she wrote: 'Something has happened which I'd like to discuss with you. As soon as you have an evening free, could you come to supper?'

CHAPTER TEN

HE CAME within hours of his return to London, ringing the doorbell while Angel and Dorothea were washing up their supper dishes.

Opening the door to him, Angel exclaimed, 'Charles! But I thought you only got back this morning?'

'I did.'

She stepped backwards to let him come in. 'Welcome home—but I hope it wasn't my note which has brought you round here so quickly. It isn't anything urgent and you must be exhausted, aren't you?'

He shook his head. 'I slept pretty well on the flight. When we landed I went straight to the bank to deal with one or two top priority matters, after which I went home and slept for three or four hours. Then I had a long shower and a shave and I'm more or less back to normal. How are you?'

'I'm fine.'

She put her hand into his, but instead of shaking it he surprised her by lifting it to his lips and kissing the backs of her fingers.

'You certainly look it. Is Dorothea in?'

'Yes, we've just finished supper. Have you eaten since you landed? Can I make you something?'

'No, thanks, not hungry. My appetite thinks it's the early hours of the morning. But I'll have a cup of coffee, if I may?'

'Of course. While you're saying hello to your aunt, I'll fetch some things from my room which I want to show you. I shan't be long.'

As she raced up the three flights of stairs to her eyrie on the top floor, her heart was bursting with joy because Charles cared enough about her to come round as soon as this. It was wonderful to have him back. Although so many exciting things had been happening to her since he left, London wasn't the same place without him. Even when she woke up in the morning knowing there was little likelihood that she would see him, she felt better knowing he was only a pigeon's flight from her than when the distance between them was a long jumbo jet flight.

When, carrying a card-stiffened manilla envelope, she joined the others, Charles said, 'Obviously I'm a bit jet-lagged. I've forgotten the presents I brought back for you both—I'm sorry about that. I'll bring them round tomorrow.'

'We're flattered that you found time to shop for us, dear boy,' said his aunt. 'Was it a successful trip?'

'Very, but I won't bore you with the details. I'm impatient to hear what it is that Angel wants to discuss. She's already talked it over with you, presumably?'

'No, I haven't told Dorothea yet,' said Angel. 'I thought I'd break it to you both at the same time. But first I'll get your coffee organised, Charles.'

'I've thought for some days that you had an air of suppressed excitement about you,' said Miss Thetford. 'But how did you know she had some-
g to tell us, Charles?'

'There was a letter from Angel waiting for me at the flat...a summons to come round post-haste.'

'Not a summons...a request,' she corrected. 'And I didn't expect to see you as soon as this. It would have kept until the end of the week.'

'But my curiosity wouldn't,' he said, smiling. 'Don't keep us in suspense. What's happened? It has to be something to do with your course, I imagine?'

'Only in the sense that it's a career opportunity, but nothing to do with catering. Have a look at these photographs.'

She opened the envelope and took out a selection of prints made from the dozens of shots Tony Sheringham had taken of her. She handed several to Dorothea and the rest to Charles, knowing that their first reaction was bound to be astonishment and wondering what their secondary reactions would be.

It was Miss Thetford who spoke first. 'Good heavens, for a moment or two I almost didn't recognise you,' she said. 'It's you...and yet it's not you. Did Tim Bolton take these, Angel?'

'No, they were taken by a man called Tony Sheringham. I shouldn't think you've ever heard of him, but he's a top fashion photographer. Tim introduced me to him. Tony thinks I could be a successful model for magazines like *Vogue* and *Harpers*.'

'*No!*'

Charles's exclamation was short, sharp and decisive. It brooked no discussion or argument. It was final; the first and last word.

'No?' his aunt echoed mildly, with a slight lift of her eyebrows. 'That's a very snap judgement, Charles. Don't you think you should hear more about it before giving your opinion?'

'I don't need to hear more about it. I don't like these pictures and from what I know about modelling it's not a suitable job for Angel,' he said, in his most adamant tone of voice.

'Why not?' asked Angel. She hadn't expected him to be in favour of it, but nor had she expected his opposition to be so immediate and arbitrary.

'Just take my word for it—it's not.' He tossed the prints on the table. 'As Aunt D. says, that's not you. It's some idiot's idea of glamour...make-up an inch thick...hair like a bird's nest...even the clothes are grotesque!'

'It's isn't the way I should want to look out of working hours, but if that's what the magazines want——' she began.

'When were those photographs taken?' he interrupted.

'One morning last week, and since then they've been seen by various art directors and fashion directors, and Tony says I can start working right away. But I wanted to talk to you first because it will make a difference to our plans for *Sea Fever*.'

'It won't make a difference to our plans because you won't be doing it,' Charles said flatly. 'I don't know why you allowed yourself to be persuaded to take part in this nonsense.'

'Charles...Charles...you're being far too scathing,' his aunt intervened, on a soothing note. 'What girl would need asking twice to have pictures

taken by a well-known fashion photographer? I
think it's very natural that Angel should have agreed
to it. She photographs terribly well, if you relate
these pictures to the sort of thing one sees in the
glossies.'

'I think they're appalling,' he said angrily, his
dark eyebrows drawing together as he looked at the
prints passed to him by Miss Thetford. 'These are
even worse than the other lot.'

'That's only your opinion,' said Angel, upset and
hurt. 'Everyone else who's seen them thinks they're
exceptionally good. Anyway, I can't see what harm
it could do for me to have a go at modelling. It's
not a commitment for life If I don't like it, I can
stop.'

'I can tell you now, you won't like it. I used to
know a model, and it isn't the glamorous life most
people imagine. It's extremely hard, boring work.'

'But also extremely well paid. According to Tony
I could earn a lot of money.'

'You don't need a lot of money. You have enough
for the present, and the prospect of earning more
doing something you like...something worthwhile, not striking ridiculous poses with a sulky
look on your face.'

'That's the expression Tony wanted. A Cheshire
Cat grin doesn't go with high fashion.'

Angel had a sudden memory of sitting cross-
legged on the deck of *Sea Fever*, a long time ago,
listening to Ludo reading *Alice in Wonderland* and
Through the Looking Glass to her. She felt h
throat thicken with tears, partly because that ha
carefree time had gone forever but mostly be
Charles was furious with her. Part of her

to placate him, but another part resented his dictatorial attitude.

'That's quite true, Charles,' said his aunt. 'The glossier the magazine, the glummer the models. It's only in the more homely magazines with knitting patterns and dresses for the fuller figure that they smile and look happy. It was just the same when I was a girl. The haughty look was in then, with plucked eyebrows and long gloves.'

Dorothea was trying to defuse an explosive situation, Angel realised. But instead of feeling grateful for the older woman's diplomatic intervention, she found herself irritated by it. What gave Charles the right to condemn the idea out of hand? Why should she kowtow to him? By all rational standards it was he who should be apologising for expressing himself too impulsively and forcefully. Why should she be denied an interesting opportunity merely because he disapproved of it?

'I'm sorry you're against it,' she said. 'But perhaps you'll change your mind when you've had as much time as I have to weigh up the pros and cons. My conclusion—after a lot more thought than you've given it—is that it's a very exciting opportunity which I'd be crazy to turn down.'

How Charles might have answered or acted had they been on their own she would never know. At that moment he looked capable of anything from tearing the prints to pieces to grabbing hold of her ‑nd shaking her.

‑Restrained by the presence of his aunt, he said ‑y, 'In that case there wasn't much point in me to come round, was there?'

His arctic glare made her chin lift defiantly. 'It was a matter of courtesy. I thought you'd be interested...pleased for me...not throw cold water on it. Well, I'm sorry you disapprove, because you've been very kind to me. But that doesn't give you the right to run my whole life for me, Charles. I'm going to have a crack at this...whether you like it or not.'

For a moment longer he stared at her. Then, with a movement of the head and shoulders which was a mixture of indifference and acquiescence, he said, 'Do whatever you wish. As you've pointed out, I have no right to interfere. You must make your own decisions. I'll see myself out.'

'Jet lag,' said Dorothea, after they had heard the front door close. 'He said he was jet lagged, and clearly he is. Laying down the law in that aggressive fashion isn't Charles's normal behaviour. I shouldn't let it worry you. He'll see your point of view when he's had a proper night's rest.'

'Will he?' Angel said doubtfully. She was remembering Leonora's warning. *Make sure you never step out of line, never answer back, never argue. If you do, you'll find yourself dropped the way I was.*

'He may never approve of your taking up fashion modelling, but I'm sure he'll concede that it's an opportunity very few if any girls would turn down,' said his aunt. 'I wouldn't myself—were I your age and had your looks.'

'The girl he mentioned...the model...did you know her?' asked Angel.

'Her name was Genia Campbell. One of grandmothers was a Russian aristocrat family had escaped being killed in the Revolution. Genia always reminded me of a borzoi, a Russian wolfhound. She gave up modelling to marry a man old enough to be her father...a Swiss banker. Charles introduced them.'

'Was Charles in love with her?'

'Not seriously. It was a long time ago. They were both in their early twenties. I should think it's years since he last gave her a thought. But these'—with a gesture at the photographs—'would naturally remind him of her. It's true that she was always complaining how tiring and boring her work was. She only did it for the money, but of course that applies to most people's attitudes to their jobs. To enjoy your way of making a living, as I do, is one of life's best and rarest gifts.'

Angel gathered the prints together and put them back in the envelope, trying not to show how deeply shaken she was by Charles's irate departure.

Was Miss Thetford right in thinking it was only because he was jet lagged that he had been so disagreeable?

At the navigation school in Devon where she took a week's refresher course before having her competence as a yachtmaster tested and certified, Angel met a man who seemed the ideal person to take charge of *Sea Fever* for her.

Her grandfather had been fifty when he had thrown up his career at the Bar. Bill Morston, the son and grandson of country solicitors, had de-
~ded to change his lifestyle at twenty-eight. He had
    nt to sail on an estuary near the small market
      where for four generations the firm of

Morston & Lyon had handled the legal affairs of the largely agricultural community.

To please his parents, Bill had followed in his father's footsteps, but had always spent every spare moment messing about in boats, latterly crewing for the owner of an ocean racer. When his younger sister had decided to qualify as a lawyer, he had realised that this released him from an obligation which he found increasingly tedious.

Bill and Angel met soon after his decision to pack up being a solicitor and make sailing his life, preferably in a part of the world where the sea was warmer and bluer than in the east coast estuary where, as a small boy in an orange life-jacket over a thick navy jersey, he had learned to handle an eight-foot dinghy.

Bill reminded Angel of her grandfather. His eyes were a paler blue and he wasn't as tall as Ludo, but he had the same easy-going, tolerant personality. She couldn't imagine him ever losing his temper. Of the group taking the course he was by far the most relaxed and good-humoured. He had also managed to pack a lot of experience into the long weekends and holidays his position as a junior partner in a family firm had allowed him.

At Miss Thetford's suggestion, Bill was invited to lunch on a Sunday convenient for Charles, whose share in the sloop entitled him to some say in who was put in charge of her.

The luncheon would be the first time Angel had seen Charles since he had stormed out of the hous and she was extremely tense and nervous about attitude to her and to Bill. She had writt Charles, explaining Bill's background qualifications, but had received no acknowledgment. The date for the two men to meet had been arranged by his aunt on the telephone.

Both men were due to arrive at the house at half-past twelve and in the preceding hour Angel changed her clothes three times, starting with an outfit which she decided was too trendy and might put his back up. She followed that with a sweater and the Spanish suede trousers, but later came to the conclusion that they were too obvious an attempt to please him.

Finally she settled for the navy blue skirt he had picked out for her at Design Thai in Bangkok and a Paisley-printed shirt she had run up on Dorothea's machine. She doubted if he would recognise the skirt. How unbelievable it would have seemed, that day he had taken her shopping, that within six months she would be starting a highly paid career as a photographic model, her first cover picture to appear on the next issue of *Vogue*.

On the stroke of twelve-thirty, someone rang the doorbell.

'I expect that's Charles . . . invariably punctual to the second. Shall I let him in or will you?' asked Miss Thetford, obviously aware that Angel was on edge about meeting him.

'I'll go,' said Angel, bracing herself.

She had been awake half the night—or so it had seemed—visualising the confrontation and re-hearsing things to say. But as she approached the ~nt door she could hear him speaking to someone, ~he opened it to find that Bill had also arrived ~e and the two men had been standing face to face on the step but now were both turning towards her.

'Hello, Angel. As you see, we've met,' said Charles, with a gesture inviting the shorter man to precede him across the threshold.

'Hello, Angel. How are you?' Bill shook hands, his amiable grin in marked contrast to the enigmatic expression on the face of the tall man behind him.

Leaving Charles to close the door, she led the way down the hall to introduce Bill to Dorothea, who greeted him warmly before lifting her cheek for her nephew's kiss.

To Angel's surprise and relief, it was soon apparent that he and Bill were going to get on with each other. She had never had any doubt of Bill's friendliness towards Charles, but had worried that her co-owner might respond with at best reserve and at worst with palpable antipathy.

However although, during lunch, Charles asked Bill a number of searching and unexpectedly knowledgeable questions, his manner was always affable, as it was towards her.

Pressed by his hostess to stay past the conventional time of departure from a lunch party, Bill didn't leave until after they had had tea and walnut cake in the garden. He was spending the night with a friend who lived in Putney, south of the river.

'You'll want to talk it over before deciding whether I'm the man for the job. But I'd be grateful if you'd let me know as soon as you can,' he said, before taking his leave.

While Charles saw him to the door, Angel collected the tea things. But when she would have carried the tray to the kitchen, Miss Thetford took it from her, saying, 'I'll deal with this while you and Charles have your discussion. You don't want to keep that nice young man in suspense a moment longer than necessary.'

They had been sitting at the far end of the long narrow London garden, and halfway to the house she met her nephew coming back and surrendered the tray to him. A few minutes later he reappeared and, with a sudden revival of apprehension, Angel watched him coming to join her for a tête-à-tête.

'As far as Bill is concerned, I don't think there's much to be said,' were his first words as he rejoined her. 'You obviously think highly of him and I'm equally favourably impressed. It was a fortunate chance that he was in Devon at the same time as you were.' He had already congratulated her on her yachtmaster's certificate.

'I'm glad you agree. In that case I'll ring him this evening at his friend's house,' said Angel.

Because he had no previous experience of chartering, and would have to pick up the necessary know-how as he went along, Bill was willing, for a couple of years, to skipper the sloop in return for no more than his keep and a modest personal allowance.

There followed a silence in which Charles watched Jacob padding along the top of one of the high brick walls which divided the garden from those next to it, and Angel watched him, feasting her eyes on the forceful profile and the mouth which, twice, had kissed hers.

When Charles turned his head to look at her, she flicked her gaze away quickly, refocusing it on the black cat, who now was almost motionless, only the end of his tail beginning to lash to and fro as he looked down at something in the garden next door.

'I don't intend,' Charles said quietly, 'to reiterate the views I expressed--perhaps rather too vigorously—the last time I was here. I'll only say that my enquiries about this man Sheringham aren't reassuring. He's given two wives grounds for divorce and a few years ago he mixed with a group of people whose parties made news when, at one of them, a girl died from a combination of drink and drugs. His professional reputation may be high, but the same can't be said of his personal standing.'

'How did you find out all this? From your ex-girlfriend, Genia Campbell?'

'She's Genia Keller now and, yes, I did give her a call to ask if she worked with Sheringham when she was modelling. She did, and never liked him. Making a pass at every good-looking girl who comes his way is routine with him, according to Genia.'

Angel didn't much like the sound of Genia Keller. Anyone who could have had Charles but had preferred to marry a rich older man saw life from a different perspective.

She said, 'Perhaps Tony Sheringham isn't as randy as he used to be. But forewarned is forearmed. I'll be ready to dodge if he looks like pouncing in my direction.'

'Do you know how?' asked Charles. 'Avoiding a determined pass isn't easy. I'm not sure you'd see it coming.'

She opened her mouth to tell him she wasn't as half-baked as he appeared to think, but the words were lost in a startled indrawing of breath as, with a single lithe movement, he rose from his chair, pulling her out of hers and into his arms.

'You see? It can happen when you least expect it. If I were Tony Sheringham how would you get out of this?' he said, holding her round the waist with one arm, the fingers of his other hand easily circling her right wrist.

'I'd probably kick you . . . him on the shin,' she said breathlessly, the unexpected close contact with his tall body making her heart behave like a trapped bird.

'Clumsy. . . and not necessarily effective. If you don't want an awkward showdown, never let things get to this stage.'

Angel looked into his eyes and smiled. 'With any other man I wouldn't.'

His fingers tightened on her wrist, communicating a tension she hadn't felt seconds earlier.

'Don't try flirting with me, Angel. You might get more than you bargained for.'

Suddenly reckless, she ran her free hand up his chest to his shoulder, feeling the latent power of well-exercised muscle under her exploring fingers.

'I might enjoy it,' she murmured, copying the mischievous glance and the play of eyelashes she had seen other girls use on men but had never tried out herself.

His arm tightened round her waist. 'You asked for this,' he said thickly, bending his head.

CHAPTER ELEVEN

IT WAS like being caught in a flash-flood, a sudden squall or the violent bursting of a dam. If he hadn't kissed her before, she would have been devastated.

What had happened the last time, in the conservatory, had prepared her a little, but it was still a shock to be kissed like this in a place which, although not precisely public, was far from being private.

For it was an extremely private kiss; the sort of kiss she had often imagined receiving, but never in a garden overlooked by many windows, to which Dorothea might return at any moment.

But Charles who, last time, had stopped kissing her the instant he realised they wouldn't be alone for much longer, seemed now not to give a damn who might be watching their embrace.

He clasped her to his hard body with almost painful strength, kissing her slowly and hungrily, leaving no doubt that what he would like to do would be to take her to bed. That message was unequivocal and Angel hoped that her response was equally clear. It was something she wanted as much as he did. If not here and now—which was manifestly impossible—as soon as it could be arranged.

She was panting and trembling and Charles, too, was breathing hard when they finally drew apar But the look in his eyes wasn't the one she ' hoped to see. Almost at once his expression '

155

to suggest that anger rather than pleasure was re-
placing passion as his dominant emotion.

'Perhaps after that you'll take my advice more
seriously,' he said brusquely.

'I always do,' she said shakily. 'Charles ... where
are you going?'

'To say goodbye to Aunt D. I must be off,' he
said over his shoulder, already striding away.

She caught up with him. 'Why must you? I—I
don't understand. A minute ago you were kissing
me, now you're rushing away!'

'It was an error of judgement. I make them like
everyone else. If you were five years older and I
were five years younger, it might not have been. As
things are, it was a mistake.'

'Last time you kissed me—before your Japanese
trip—you said you hoped I would miss you. You
implied you were going to miss me.'

'And came back to find you over the moon about
your new career,' he reminded her curtly. 'You
didn't take my advice about that, did you?'

'No, but I did think it over. I didn't just ignore
it. Are you still angry about it?'

He stopped short, and turned to face her. 'Not
angry ... merely concerned that you shouldn't be
spoiled or corrupted by people who don't value
innocence and sweetness. I'd like you to stay as you
are.'

Before Angel could reply to this, Miss Thetford
appeared in the doorway of the conservatory.
'Telephone for you, Angel ... Carol.'

Cursing Carol, a fellow student on the catering
ourse, for picking this inopportune time to ring
Angel hurried through to the kitchen. Unfor-
ely Carol was a chatterbox who, when her

parents were out, made long calls to her friends and had several urgent things to say, even though Angel told her this wasn't a convenient moment for a long gossip.

Short of ringing off while the other girl was in mid-sentence, there was nothing Angel could do but stem the flow as soon as possible. But by that time Charles had gone, his farewell being an avuncular pat on her shoulder in passing, as if the heart-churning embrace in the garden had never happened.

She found it hard to sleep that night. Charles had aroused deep longings which no doubt would die down eventually but tonight would not let her rest. She tossed and turned, aching to be in his arms, in his bed. He was the only man she wanted to make love to her, ever. But clearly he had scruples about becoming her lover. Which could only mean that, although he found her physically desirable, he didn't love her in the way she loved him—wholly, completely, forever.

Why should he? She wasn't old enough, didn't know enough, to be worthy of him. Yet Leonora had implied that it was her immaturity, her mal-leability, which appealed to him.

Two nights later she went to his flat.

Dorothea had gone to a concert with Ralph Kingsland, thinking Angel intended to watch a film about Indonesia on television. But soon after they had left the house, she programmed Miss Thetford's video to record the film for her and took a taxi to the Barbican. There was every possib' that Charles would be out when she got ther at least she would know where he lived and the colour of his front door.

'Angel! What are you doing here?' were his first words, when he opened it.

'Are you busy? May I come in?'

He stepped back to allow her to enter. For a second—but only a second—he had seemed to be pleased to see her. Now his face had resumed the expression she was never able to read.

'What brings you to this end of town?' he demanded.

'An impulse. Dorothea is out with Ralph, and I was feeling lonely. I thought I'd come and see you. You don't mind, I hope?'

He avoided a direct answer by saying, 'I might have been out. You could have saved a wasted journey by ringing up first.'

Angel unbuttoned her windcheater. 'If I had, you'd have put me off... wouldn't you?'

He didn't answer that either. Helping her take off the jacket, he said, 'Have you ever tried apple tea? The woman who stocks my freezer came back from Turkey last week and she brought me a jar of Oralet. I was just going to make a cup of the stuff.'

Tossing her jacket on a chair, he led the way to his kitchen which, compared with his aunt's, was a place of soulless efficiency, more like an operating theatre than the heart of a home.

The electric kettle switched itself off as they entered. Charles produced a second mug, tipped in spoonfuls of pale grains and added hot water.

'The taste is a bit synthetic, but it makes a change instant coffee.' He carried the mugs to a breakfast counter and, having placed them on top, drew out two tall chrome stools.

Before perching on one, Angel said, 'Am I not to be allowed to see your sitting-room?'

It crossed her mind that he might already have a visitor; one he didn't want her to meet, or to meet her. It was agony to wonder if, so soon after kissing her, he was entertaining someone who would be spending the night here.

But there was no hesitation or embarrassment in his reply, 'Of course, if you want to.'

A few moments later, looking round his large, comfortable, modern sitting-room, she regretted her suspicions. Clearly he had been spending the evening working. Through the open door of an adjoining study, she could see the monitor of a computer with a complicated chart showing on the screen.

'Oh, dear, you were working. I've disturbed you. Why didn't you say so?'

'I'm usually working. It isn't anything urgent. Sit down and tell me why you were lonely. I thought you had several girl friends if you needed company. What about the girl who rang up on Sunday... Carol, was it?'

'Yes, Carol—what an excellent memory you have!—but I wasn't in the mood for a natter with her this evening. I wanted to talk to you... about Sunday.'

At his suggestion Angel had seated herself, but Charles was still on his feet and now walked away towards the window which, his flat being a penthouse, had a wide view of London's old and new rooftops.

'What about Sunday?' he asked, standing with his back to her.

She moistened her lips with a sip of the hot apple tea. 'Charles, that's the third time you've kissed me . . . which suggests that you rather like doing it. I like it too . . . very much. I'd like to . . . to go all the way.'

He swung round, visibly staggered. She had never expected to see him flummoxed by anyone, least of all by her.

Seizing her momentary advantage, she said, 'You said you didn't want me to change. But I can't stay a virgin much longer. Wouldn't it be better for you to make love to me than, say, someone like Tim who may not be very good at it?'

Charles had recovered himself. He said, with an incisive snap, 'It would be better if you stuck to your original plan to stay out of men's beds until you find someone you want to share everything with. Is Tim trying to persuade you to have an affair with him?'

'No, he isn't. Nobody is. But I'm ready for love . . . ripe for it. In the East girls much younger than I am are married with children.'

'Because it's their only option. In the West, if they have any sense, girls mature before they get married.'

'But they don't wait until they marry to find out about making love. Why must I? I'm curious . . . longing to know if it's all it's cracked up to be. Why can't you show me?'

'For God's sake, Angel——' he began. Then words seemed to fail him and he put down his mug and strode past her into the next room.

From where she was sitting she could see him remove a disk from a slot under the screen and put it away in a case. Then he touched a switch and the screen went blank.

Returning to the sitting-room, he said, 'Come on: I'm taking you home.'

'But I don't want to go home.'

'And how do you think Aunt D. would feel if she came home and found you missing? Or haven't you thought about that?'

She hadn't, for the simple reason that when she set out it hadn't been her intention to offer herself to him.

'Obviously not,' said Charles. 'Clearly you haven't thought this crazy idea through at all. You can try apple tea another time.' He took the mug from her hand, set it down and yanked her ungently to her feet, before hustling her back to the hall. There he bundled her into her jacket before taking a light raincoat from a cupboard and his latch-key from the hall table. Moments later they were on their way down to ground level.

Angel had thought he might put her into a taxi, give her address to the driver and send her home by herself. But he came with her.

As the taxi sped along High Holborn, at this hour clear of its heavy daytime traffic, Angel sat in her corner and wondered what had possessed her to make such a fool of herself. At the time it had seemed a good idea to take the initiative. Now it seemed an act of madness.

Inwardly cringing with embarrassment, but determined not to let him know it, she gathered th rags of her self-possession around her, saying, 'T way you rushed me out of your flat was almost panic-stricken, Charles. One wouldn't expect you to flap at being propositioned.'

He leaned forward to close the sliding glass panel behind the driver's seat. But all he said was, 'I'm not superhuman, Angel.'

What did that mean? That he had been tempted? That he wanted her so badly that he couldn't trust himself to be alone with her? She wished she could believe it, but a more likely explanation was that since he had—as far as they knew—no regular girl-friend at present, any willing woman was a temptation to him.

Suddenly he stretched out his hand and took hers, holding it loosely on the leather seat between them.

'If you were a little older...twenty...twenty-one...I wouldn't be taking you home,' he said. 'Or if I were ten years younger and women were still playthings to me. But that's over...that stage of my life. One grows out of light love affairs. They're like discos, they lose their appeal—except to people who suffer from arrested development,' he added drily.

Angel thought: I shall remember this moment for the rest of my life. The feel of Charles's hand holding mine.

She said, 'I think my problem is accelerated development; perhaps because of growing up with Ludo. I generally feel more comfortable with older people than with my contemporaries. They often seem childish to me.'

'In some ways you are more mature than most people of your age,' he agreed. 'But life is full of wonderful experiences, Angel. You don't have to ▾ them all at once. Save making love for later. If you try it merely out of curiosity, you'll be disappointed.'

She nerved herself to say, 'Not with you. I know that by what happens to me when you kiss me. Please, Charles... won't you reconsider?'

For a moment his fingers tightened in a grip which made her knuckle-bones crunch. He said abruptly, 'There's only one circumstance in which I would make love to you... if we were married. Is your curiosity so great that you'll commit the rest of your life to me to satisfy it?'

Was he serious? Was this a proposal? Or was it a sardonic joke? Confused and uncertain, she searched his face for the meaning behind his extra-ordinary statement.

Still unsure of her ground, her heart pounding with nervous excitement, she answered him with a question. 'What would you do if I said yes?'

For an instant she saw in his eyes—or thought she saw—the look which had been there before he kissed her in the garden a few days ago. But this time it wasn't followed by a ravenous kiss. Instead he let go of her hand and folded his arms across his chest, perhaps to stop himself reaching for her or perhaps because it was one of his most charac-teristic postures.

'I should suggest that we talk about this again in, say, a year's time.'

'Ralph has asked me to marry him and I've said I will,' Miss Thetford announced at breakfast the following morning.

'Oh, that's wonderful... I'm so glad!' A jumped up to dart round the table and hug

'Thank you, my dear...so am I,' said the older woman, beaming. 'I didn't think it was possible to fall in love at my age, but it seems that it is. I lay awake half the night, thinking about him and how lucky I am to have met him.'

Angel had also lain awake, but for reasons very different from the happy cause of Dorothea's insomnia. Had Charles proposed to her or hadn't he? She still wasn't sure. But even if he had been serious, there was no way his offer could be construed as a declaration of love.

'Don't worry. This doesn't mean that you'll have nowhere to live,' said Miss Thetford. 'We're going to be married almost immediately, but I shan't be moving to Ralph's house in Harley Street. That's really only a bachelor flat above the consulting-rooms he shares with another specialist. When his first wife was alive, he spent every weekend at their country house, but it was sold after she died—he found it too large and too lonely without her, so he's going to come and live here and let his children have his flat as a pied-à-terre.'

'But you won't want me playing gooseberry,' said Angel, using one of the old-fashioned expressions learnt from Ludo which sometimes puzzled people of her own age. 'I must find a pad of my own.'

'No, no, Ralph would be most upset if he felt he'd driven you out. He knows I regard you as my adopted granddaughter and he's very fond of you too. The thing is, shall you mind being here alone while we're on our honeymoon? We're going round the world for six months. Although we've both travelled fairly widely, there are lots of places we haven't seen and we want to visit them together, before we get old and infirm.'

As she spoke, Dorothea's happiness and excitement made her look years younger than her actual age. Angel felt deeply envious; she couldn't imagine anything more blissful than a six-month journey to faraway places with Charles. But somehow she couldn't see him taking a long break from banking to go on an extended honeymoon. He had told her that one day, when he had enough money, he would get out of the rat race, but would that day ever come? Would he be happy without the power and influence he wielded at present? It didn't seem likely.

After their mid-morning register office wedding, Professor and Mrs Ralph Kingsland gave a lunch party at the Savoy Hotel before flying to Paris for a few days, their long wedding trip being postponed until later in the year when they would have fulfilled various existing commitments.

Before they set out on their travels it was arranged that, while they were away, Angel would share the house with Hilary, a schoolfriend of Ralph's elder daughter. Hilary was thirty-eight, had recently left her husband and wanted to work in London where she had lived before her marriage to a Fenland farmer. It appeared to have been a case of a consuming attraction which for a time had obscured the fact that they had nothing else in common. Hilary had been unhappy in the flat, windswept emptiness of the Fens and her husband had been disappointed when they failed to have the children he wanted.

By the time Hilary moved in, Angel's career as a photographic model had already begun to take off. The money which Charles had paid for share of *Sea Fever*—which had seemed a lot at the time—might, it seemed, soon be exceeded by her own startling earnings.

Ralph and Dorothea had been overseas for three months, and were planning to spend Christmas in New Zealand, when her career took on a new dimension. An appearance on an early-morning chat show led to an invitation to stand in, at the last moment, for a well-known actress who was one of the regulars on a panel game.

Angel's role, she suspected, was to look decorative and leave most of the talking to the two males on the team, one an egghead, the other a wit. However, it happened that the first question she was asked was on a subject connected with one of Ludo's best jokes. She told it, and brought the house down. The studio audience roared and the two men on either side of her, whose manner before the show started had been faintly patronising, joined in the laughter and looked at her with more respect.

The show was screened a week later and the following night Hilary, who still had many friends in London, gave a party. As the women on her guest list outnumbered the men, she had turned to Angel for help with balancing the numbers. Angel had asked Tim Bolton, Tony Sheringham and Charles, all of whom had said they would come.

'Saw you on TV last night. You were terrific,' said Tim, when he arrived. 'Have they asked you to go on again?'

'As a matter of fact they have. But it was only luck that I knew the answers. Next time I may not now any.'

'Doesn't matter, if you can make people laugh.'

'I can't. Those were Ludo's jokes... don't you remember? I'm sure he must have told them while you were with us.'

'Maybe... it's a long time ago. Anyway, you had everyone on the floor last night, or whenever it was the show was recorded.'

Tony, who had also watched the screening, was more guarded in his approval. 'You were a hit, but TV's a tricky medium. It doesn't take long to build someone into a nationally-known "personality", but there's always a danger of overkill, and once that happens you're finished forever,' he warned. 'If I were you I'd stay off the small screen until you've run out of mileage as a model.'

He looked round the room, noticed Hilary and asked, 'Who's that?'

Angel took him across and introduced him. Contrary to Charles's forecast, Tony had never made advances to her. He used language which made her wince and had no manners to speak of, but whatever he had been like in Genia's time as a model, he no longer made passes at random. But the way he was looking at Hilary when Angel left them together, it seemed probable he might try one later.

Knowing, because she had said so, that Hilary was looking for an unattached man who would give her a good time in and out of bed without any of the penalties she associated with marriage, Angel hoped her co-hostess wouldn't let Tony stay the night. She felt certain that Ralph and Dorothea would disapprove, not only because they had the moral standards of their generation but becaus Tony was a chain-smoker and, if he spent mu time here, would soon have every room in the house reeking of cigarettes.

Charles was the last to arrive. He had come to the house for the Kingslands' farewell party, and been introduced to Hilary, but since then Angel hadn't seen him, although they had talked on the telephone about the investment of her modelling fees.

It was a cold night, and when she opened the front door, he was standing on the step beginning to unbutton a navy blue overcoat. A long scarf, cashmere on one side and dark Paisley silk on the other, was tied round his neck. The rims of his ears and his cheekbones had been reddened by the cold, but she knew he had been back to Bali a few weeks earlier and his skin had its usual tan, making everyone else, including herself, look winter-pale by comparison.

'I was beginning to think you couldn't make it,' she said, offering her hand but not her cheek.

He stepped into the house. In spite of the freezing air outside, his ungloved fingers were warm as they closed over hers.

'Sorry I'm late—got held up at the office. Congratulations on your performance last night. As *The Times* critic said this morning, you lit up that rather stale show like a sparkler on a party pudding.'

'You watched it?' said Angel, pleased. She had told him she was going to be on, but she hadn't felt sure he would watch.

'I was out last night, so I taped it and saw it this morning. I clipped *The Times*' notice for you in ~~se~~ you hadn't seen it.' He handed her an envelope.

~~ink~~ you.' She put it in the pocket of her full taffeta skirt. 'Let me take your coat.'

'Don't you want to read it now?'

'First things first...you must need a reviver after a long busy day. Come and have a rum punch and a hot mince pie to keep you going until supper is served.'

As she hung his coat on a peg, Charles asked, 'Have you made any plans for Christmas?'

Angel's heart leapt, then plummeted. Hilary was spending Christmas with her brother and his wife. Thinking it a vain hope that Charles would want to include her in his arrangements, Angel had accepted an invitation to spend the holiday with Carol and her family. Now she wished she hadn't. It would have been better to risk spending Christmas alone than to miss the chance to be with him. Unfortunately the principles Ludo had drummed into her from early childhood made it impossible to deny that she had any plans.

All she could do was say, 'Carol's parents keep open house for anyone who's on their own. I said I'd go there, but——'

'That's fine,' Charles cut in briskly. 'I'm going to be in America, but I would have fixed you up with friends of mine if you'd had none of your own to spend the festivities with. Now lead me to that rum punch!'

CHAPTER TWELVE

SEEING *Sea Fever* lying at anchor off Tobago, Angel's eyes filled with tears.

It seemed such a long, long time since she had last seen the sloop. Far longer than two years.

In some ways those years had sped as the pace of her career had accelerated. But always, deep in her heart, there had been an aching longing for the life she had lived with Ludo; the unhurried, carefree days and quiet nights of the time before fame and fortune had come upon her.

She still went to bed at an hour which would have surprised those who visualised her private life as a succession of parties or dinners *à deux* at fashionable restaurants. But early nights were almost the only resemblance between her past and her present. Early nights; and the fact that she always went to bed alone, still saving herself for Charles, who didn't appear to want her.

Bill Morston, who had met her at the airport, said, 'She looks good, doesn't she? Better than the new sloops without bowsprits and topsails.'

'She looks wonderful,' Angel said huskily.

She had flown from London to Trinidad the week before on a modelling assignment, her first one in the Caribbean and also her first opportunity to ¬pend a few days on *Sea Fever* while no one else ¬s on board except Bill and his crew, a girl called ¬e who also cooked for the charter parties.

This morning, her assignment completed, Angel had flown the short distance from Trinidad to Tobago, where a bronzed and fit-looking Bill had been waiting to take the roll-bag which was her only luggage.

'I thought you would have changed a lot, but you seem just the same,' he remarked, as they climbed into the sloop's tender.

'You should have seen me yesterday, flouncing around the Trinidad Hilton in the latest resort wear with a ton of make-up on my face!' said Angel, with a grin.

Now she was wearing pale blue jeans, white loafers and a plain white T-shirt and her long hair was plaited for coolness. Without make-up or jewellery, she was hardly recognisable as the sophisticated model—soon to turn TV presenter—of yesterday.

Photographs of *Sea Fever*'s refit had prepared her for the changes she would find between decks. But before Bill took her below to see the luxurious alterations which had brought the sloop up to the standard demanded by the rich people who chartered her for their holidays, he introduced Josie, a small but sturdy brunette with short hair and a gap between her front teeth.

One of the drawbacks of her job, Angel had found out, was that she often received hostile vibes from other women, particularly those who were self-conscious about their physical shortcomings. But although Josie was rather plain with short legs and solid hips, there was nothing unfriendly in her manner. She exuded good humour and capability.

'We've put you in one of the double cabins,' she said. 'Would you like a swim before lunch?'

'Oh, yes, please—that would be heaven,' Angel said eagerly.

She followed Josie below to a cabin no longer recognisable as the shabby one her grandfather had occupied.

They had lunch on deck, under the smart new awning at a table laid in the style known as Rustic Chic with food to match; the chilled Spanish soup called *gazpacho*, which Josie had learned to make while crewing in the Mediterranean, followed by a decorative salad, followed by fruit.

Half a bottle of champagne, shared with Josie while Bill drank lager, made Angel feel drowsy afterwards. She didn't drink much as a rule, but Bill had opened the champagne to celebrate her return to her former home and she hadn't demurred when he had twice refilled her glass.

'Why don't you take a nap?' Josie suggested, when Angel suppressed her third yawn.

'Do you know, I think I will. I expect it's partly the heat which is making me tired—I haven't got acclimatised yet. But don't let me sleep too long. I'm only here for five days, I don't want to waste time snoozing.'

When she woke, she knew by the much lower angle of the sun that it was past the time when Josie had promised to call her.

In the saloon, she found a note on the table.

'Gone ashore. Not sure when we'll be back but no doubt you'll be glad to have S F to yourself for a while. B.'

Angel *was* pleased to be on her own for a time, ~~b~~ut she thought it odd they hadn't mentioned ~~go~~ing to go ashore again. Neither of them seemed

the sort of person who would forget to buy some
vital supply. Perhaps it was fish they were after.
During lunch Josie had mentioned that the local
fishermen sold their catches late in the afternoon,
but she hadn't said she was planning to have fish
for dinner tonight.

Less than an hour later, while she was looking
at a chart of the bays and reefs surrounding the
island, Angel heard the drone of an outboard motor
and went to see if it was the others returning or a
passing islander.

It was a tender identical to the sloop's which she
saw when she stepped on deck, but the man at the
tiller was alone, and he wasn't Bill. At first she took
him for a stranger. Then as the dinghy came nearer
and she saw who it was, her jaw dropped in as-
tounded recognition.

'*Charles!*' she whispered incredulously.

'Hello, Angel. How are you? Long time no see, as
they say.' He tossed up a nylon roll-bag as lightly
packed as her own.

She didn't respond to his greeting. 'What are you
doing here?' she demanded.

'The same as you...taking time off from the rat-
race. When Bill told me you were coming, it seemed
an opportune moment for me to fly out as well.'

Her heart had begun to fibrillate. 'Where is Bill?
How will he and Josie get back?'

Having made fast the dinghy, Charles turned to
her and said calmly, 'They'll be spending the night
at Richmond Great House, a two-hundred-year-old
plantation house on the Atlantic side of the island.
It belongs to a Tobagonian who's a professor
Columbia University, New York. When he's

using the house, he lets visitors use it. Bill and Josie are spending the second week of their honeymoon there. They were married last Wednesday morning but agreed to stay on board until you and I arrived.'

'They're married! Why didn't they tell me?'

'I asked them not to. I wanted to surprise you.'

'You can say that again!' Angel retorted. 'I hope, during this conspiracy, you also arranged for a helmsman and cook to replace them. I'm here to take it easy.'

'So you shall. But would it be too much to ask you to fix me a long cold drink while I take a quick shower? They've put you in the green cabin and me in the blue, I believe.' Charles headed for the hatchway, saying over his shoulder, 'And a slug of rum in my drink, please.'

His absence gave Angel a chance to pull herself together and consider the implications of the arrangements he and Bill had made behind her back. But her mind was still in a state of considerable confusion when he reappeared.

'I—I wasn't sure how long you'd be and I didn't want the ice to have melted before you were ready,' she said, to explain why so far all she had done was to locate the tall, heavy-bottomed glasses intended for long drinks.

'Having been out here before, I make a pretty good rum punch. Will you join me?' he asked.

'Yes, but don't make it too strong. I've already had half a bottle of champagne with my lunch.'

'Then perhaps you'd better stick to mineral water. I don't want you to nod off again. When they met me at the airport, Josie said they'd left you in a deep sleep and you might not be awake when I got
'

'I'd been up for some time. Thank you.' Angel took the glass of iced water he handed her, and sipped it while he poured some dark rum into his own glass. 'Do you mind telling me how we're going to manage without them?'

'I have another surprise for you. Now *I* have a yachtmaster's certificate. Helped by a lad who'll be coming on board when we go ashore for dinner, I shall sail *Sea Fever*. All you have to do is to make your own breakfast.'

'Who's going to cook all the other meals?'

'Don't worry, it won't be you. Most of the time we'll eat out at the island's hotels. Let's go on deck again, shall we . . . watch the sun go down?'

'Are you serious about being a certified yacht-master?' she asked, when they were both reclining on the comfortably padded fold-up loungers which Bill had put out before he left.

'Of course. I wouldn't be here if I weren't . . . or not without Bill as skipper. I've never been the reckless type. If I'm going to take charge of a valuable boat and a girl who's been offered a headline-making TV contract, I need to know what I'm doing. And I do. As well as knowing all the theory, I've picked up a lot of experience, some of it in quite hairy conditions. Every spare day I've had has been spent on deck off the south coast, or in the North Sea or somewhere. Weekends and holidays as well.'

'You've kept it very quiet,' she said. 'Even your aunt has no idea all this has been going on.'

'I've always kept my cards close to my chest,' he answered. 'So do you, for that matter. I didn't know you'd been offered the job of presenter of a peak-hour show until I read it in the paper. I

it you won't resist an offer as tempting as that?—
or were the Press exaggerating the size of the
salary?'

'No, they weren't. It's a lot of money...but I
haven't made up my mind yet. That's why I wanted
this break. To think things out...decide where my
future lies.'

Charles tilted his glass to take a long swig of his
drink. His hair, still wet from the shower, was
sticking together in strands which as they dried
would separate and become a thick, soft, dense
mass. Angel felt an impulse to touch the parts of
his cheeks now faintly shadowed and probably due
to be shaved before they went out to dinner.

He said, 'You may not remember, but a long time
ago we were talking in Aunt D's garden and you
quoted Wordsworth to me. "Getting and spending,
we lay waste our powers." I've decided the moment
has come when I've had enough getting and
spending. It's time for a simpler life. So where my
own future lies is here, on board *Sea Fever*...unless
you have some objection?'

Not wholly clear what he meant, Angel said,
'What about Bill and Josie?'

'They'd like to set up on their own and I'm prepared to finance them at a less swingeing rate of
interest than they'd have to pay on a bank loan.
Bill's seen a boat he fancies at a price he considers
reasonable. As soon as it's fit for service, I shall
take over here. I've already drafted my letter of res-
ignation from Cornwall Chester. It's on my computer, waiting to be printed and signed.'

'Are you planning to carry on chartering?'

'That depends. Possibly...if I can find a cook-
-crew as good as Josie.' As the sun sank below

the horizon he peered at his watch. 'Time we were getting ready. On Bill's recommendation, I've booked a table at the Kariwak Village.'

Angel went below and had a shower and washed her hair. As she dried it, she thought about all the men who had been interested in her but whom she had always discouraged because from the day they had met she had cared only for this man. But now her delight at Charles's arrival was mixed with anger and resentment because of the pain he had caused her.

Had she been dining on board, she would have left her hair loose and put on jeans and a shirt. Not knowing how glamorous a place the Kariwak would be, she decided to put her hair up and to wear a simple black and white shift. She had bought it at the boutique in the Trinidad Hilton where she and the rest of the *Harpers & Queen* party had been staying as guests of the management for whom the feature on resort clothes would be a good advertisement.

'Amazing,' said Charles, when she joined him in the saloon and he scanned the hairdo, the dress and the high-heeled sandals she was dangling by their sling-backs.

'What's amazing?'

'The speed of your transformation.'

'It would have been quicker, but I had to wash the salt out of my hair.'

Evidently the place where they were dining didn't have too strict a dress code. Charles was wearing white denim trousers and loafers with a short-sleeved navy blue shirt with the collar butto undone.

He was rubbing some liquid from a bottle on to his sinewy, lightly haired forearms. 'Have you anti-mozzed your legs?' he asked. 'According to Josie they're the most vulnerable parts. Mosquitoes lurk under tables, especially out-of-doors tables.'

Two years in a temperate climate hadn't made Angel forget the precautions necessary in the tropics. She had already used an insect repellent in stick form, like solid cologne. But he wasn't to know that.

She said, 'That stuff looks oily, I don't want it on my hands. Would you put some on for me, please?'

She lifted a long bare leg, resting her foot on the end of the C-shaped banquette behind the oval table. Yesterday her toenails had been dark red, the colour chosen by the fashion stylist. Now they were painted with the natural varnish she preferred.

Charles dribbled a little of the lotion on to her shin and rubbed it in.

'It isn't as sticky as it looks. In a few minutes' time you won't know it's there.'

The feel of his palm stroking from the back of her ankle, up her calf to behind her knee, made her tremble inwardly. She wanted to close her eyes and revel in his touch, but she kept them open and, when he had done one leg, lifted the other. Did touching her have the same effect on him as it did on her? It was impossible to tell.

Her dress was sleeveless, high at the front but low at the back.

'Better have some on your arms,' he said.

She had asked for this delicious torture, Angel thought, as he rubbed the stuff on her arms. She had never tried aromatherapy, disliking the idea of

being massaged by another woman. Performed by
Charles, aromatherapy would be heaven. The mere
thought of his strong, gentle hands on the covered
parts of her body made her shake and quiver inside.
Even now, with him stroking her spine, it took all
her self-control not to groan with sheer sensuous
pleasure.

'This stuff has a bitter taste if it gets on one's
lips. I'll wash my hands and then we'll be off.'

His voice sounded slightly husky and he went to
his cabin rather than into the galley, making her
wonder if, had she thought to look, she might have
seen conclusive evidence that touching her had
aroused him as strongly as she was aroused.

When the dinghy arrived at the place where they
were to meet the crew Bill had hired to help Charles
and mind the sloop in their absence, waiting for
them was a taxi-driver and a tall West Indian youth
with a grin as white as his T-shirt in the moonlight,
and a pair of sneakers slung round his neck by their
laces.

Charles had already rolled up the legs of his
trousers. When he had cut the motor and tilted it
inboard, and after the dinghy had glided by its own
momentum into shallow water, he threw his loafers
on to the beach, slid his long legs over the side and
held out his arms to Angel.

Still having her shoes in her hand, she wouldn't
have minded getting her feet and ankles wet. But
she put an arm round his neck and subsided in
his arms, remembering how, the week before
had been photographed in the arms of a male
without feeling anything like the sensation

coursed through her now as Charles carried her ashore.

The lanky boy's name was Lester and, obviously knowing the drill, he filled a bailer with water and sluiced the sand from the Englishman's feet which Charles dried on a towel kept in the dinghy for that purpose.

Then Lester boarded the dinghy, promising to come back for them at half-past ten, and they followed the driver up the beach to his car, parked by a line of coconut palms.

At the Kariwak, they were shown to a table in one of the two octagonal palm-thatched enclosures with rustic balustrades which stood between the bar and the chevron-shaped swimming pool. This was lit by underwater lights which also illuminated the surrounding garden and nine octagonal cabins which formed the Kariwak's 'village'.

The tables were fairly close together and Angel would have preferred to dine in greater seclusion. But it was soon apparent that most of the other diners were staying at the hotel and forming holiday friendships. Plenty of table-to-table chatter about where to go and what to see made it unlikely that anyone would overhear what she and Charles were saying to each other.

After a tall, slender waitress in a full skirt and ruffled cotton blouse had recited the menu and taken their order, he said, 'So you haven't decided whether to start a new career as a TV presenter. What's holding you back?'

The table was lit by a candle inside an amber
~m-glass. Angel looked at the flame, not at him,
~ answered, 'Mainly the fact that I'm not very
'n my present career. TV would be more

interesting than modelling, I suppose, but basically I'd be exchanging one type of studio for another. The fashion scene and television are both man-made worlds . . . totally artificial. I think I belong in the natural world of wind and water and sunlight.' She raised her eyes to his face. 'Where do you think I belong?'

Without hesitation, he said, 'I think you belong on *Sea Fever*. If you hadn't run into Tim Bolton, you'd have come back to her long before this.'

'If I hadn't run into you, I might never have left her,' she said. 'Or I might have lost her forever.'

The waitress came back with their first course and the bottle of wine Charles had ordered.

When she had gone, ignoring the food set before him, he said, 'Perhaps I've lost you. Have I, Angel?'

She broke the home-made brown roll on her side plate. 'I don't understand that question. I was never yours to lose.'

'You wanted to be mine.'

She made an airy gesture with her hand. 'That was ages ago. Rather ungentlemanly of you to remind me of my youthful follies, don't you think?'

She was going to leave it at that, but suddenly changed her mind and, leaning towards him, speaking in a lower voice, said, 'It's not important any more, but have you any idea how much pain you caused me at the time, Charles?'

'No more pain than I felt myself,' he said, with a twisted smile. 'But the difference between love and desire is that love wants what's best for the other person. You were too young then. You had to have time to grow up and do your own thing. If you'd jumped at the idea of marrying me, I would have weakened. But you didn't.'

'Jumped at an offer of marriage with no mention of love! What woman would?' she retorted.

'The fact that I was taking you home should have told you something,' he said drily.

The waitress hovered beside them. 'You don't like the fish mousse?' she asked, her expression concerned.

'I'm sure it's delicious. We were so busy talking, we forgot to start eating,' explained Angel. She tried a mouthful. 'Mm . . . it's excellent.'

'It wasn't a good idea to come here,' said Charles, when the girl had left them. 'We should have had pot luck on board and thrashed all this out in private.'

She made a pretence of eating the mousse with enjoyment. 'Thrashed what out?'

'The future . . . whether we're going to spend it together. I didn't spell it out before, but I will now. I love you. I want to marry you. But you're still very young to settle down. If you want to try the TV job, that would be OK by me. I could carry on at C.C. until you'd got it out of your system. I know I've sometimes laid down the law in the past, but only because you seemed so innocent and vulnerable. If we were married, I would never want to curb you.'

He still hadn't touched his mousse and although it was very good, the thought of the main course and pudding made her say, 'Oh, Charles, let's get out of here. It really is quite impossible to discuss our personal affairs with all these people around us. Say you're not well or something. Tell them we'll come back another evening.'

*   *   *

The taxi had not brought them far, and walking at this time of night was not like walking by day when the heat of the sun was so strong that it made the sand feel like a hot-plate.

Near the hotel was a main road and, beyond it, a quiet by-road crossing some parched common land where a few scraggy cattle were tethered.

Charles hadn't spoken since they had left the Kariwak and Angel knew it was up to her to make the next move. She slipped her hand into his.

'My feelings haven't changed. I still feel the same as I did the night I came to your flat,' she told him.

He had been shortening his stride to match her pace in high heels. Now, coming abruptly to a standstill, he swung to face her.

'Are you sure?'

'I was sure then...even before that. I was sure the first time we met. I knew you were someone special.'

He must have been holding his breath. It came out in a long, deep sigh.

'So was I...and I thought I'd gone mad. Oh, God, Angel...darling...at last!'

An instant later she was locked in his arms, being kissed with a pent-up passion which felt like being swept overboard by a giant wave, except that would have been terrifying and this was wonderful.

Laughter and lewd remarks from a passing car reminded them where they were. In the shelter of Charles's strong arms Angel felt totally safe, but she did wonder for a moment if warnings about Trinidad applied to its much smaller neighbour. But from what she had seen of Tobago it had a quiet, rural air, quite different from Port of Spain where wandering around after dark was said to be asking for trouble.

Anyway, Charles seemed unworried and, remembering his over-anxious attitude to her safety in London, she felt sure he wouldn't have suggested walking back to the beach if he hadn't already checked out the situation here with Bill.

As they strolled on, she said, 'If you want to know the reason why I didn't jump at your first proposal, it was because of Leonora. After you'd broken up, she and I met in the street. She guessed how I felt about you, and she told me you would never find a woman to match up to your ideal, but because I was young and malleable, you might try to make me fit your blueprint.'

'Never heard such rubbish!' was his comment. 'She was jealous of you, and with reason. We broke up because, for the first time in my life, I'd discovered what love was all about. Incidentally, in case you're wondering, there's been no one else since Leonora.'

'No one at all?'

'No one.'

'That's a very long time to be celibate,' said Angel, knowing he was speaking the truth and wondering how many men would deny themselves the solace of someone's embrace if for any reason the woman they really wanted was unattainable. It made her realise, more than ever, what a strong, staunch character he was.

'But at least you knew what you were missing, which is more than I did . . . or do. As you told me that night in the taxi, life isn't a bargain basement where you have to grab something or miss it. I'm still waiting for you to introduce me to that particular pleasure, Charles.'

He stopped and pulled her against him. 'Which I shall be happy to do the moment we've got rid of Lester.'

Since the sloop was moored quite far out, she was doubtful that Charles's bellowed ahoys would attract their sitter's attention. But at the third yell he appeared and was soon on his way to fetch them.

'We've had a change of plan, Lester. We're going to stay here tomorrow, so we won't need you till the day after...and not too early in the morning. Say around ten?'

'Sure, man. No problem.' Lester thanked Charles for the notes which had changed hands, said, 'G'night, ma'am,' to Angel, and sauntered off to the road with the springy, almost-dancing gait she had first noticed among the young men of Trinidad.

On the way back to the sloop, Charles said, 'Do you have to go back on Friday? Couldn't you stay on longer?'

'No, I have to work on Monday,' she told him regretfully. 'You know I should love to stay, but at least we have these few days and it won't be long before we're together for life.'

'We're together for life as from now. If you have commitments next week, I'll come back to London with you.'

'I wonder what Dorothea will say. I've never confided in her, but I think she must have guessed how I felt about you.'

'She knew how I felt about you. I told her...asked her advice.'

'Which was?'

'That I had nothing to worry about. She thought we were made for each other... regardless of the age difference. I had only to wait until you were a little older.'

'Which you have and I am and here we are... home at last,' said Angel, as they circled *Sea Fever*'s stern because she had swung with the tide and now was lying with her bowsprit pointing out to sea, as if poised to start her next voyage.

For the second time that day Charles made fast the dinghy and then caught Angel in his arms and continued the kisses cut short on the road across the common.

'I think we'd better go below,' he said thickly, a few moments later. 'Your cabin or mine?'

'Yours.'

Her hand in his, he led the way down the companion ladder and through the saloon where, earlier, she had wondered if touching her had aroused him. That was no longer in doubt. Her only uncertainty now was whether her theoretical knowledge of how to make love to a man would counterbalance her lack of experience. She wanted terribly to please him, to make up for all the lonely nights when he had needed her and she hadn't been there. She would never forget the bleak look in his eyes when she had accused him of causing her pain, and the wry grimace which had accompanied his answer.

Moonlight was flooding his starboard cabin, and silvery sequin-like patterns made by reflections from the sea shimmered on the deck-head. Her cabin, on the port side, would be in shadow until the tide changed. This was not why she had chosen his cabin for their first night together, but it pleased her that she would be able to see as well as feel Charles making love to her.

He drew her in and closed the door. As she felt for the pins which anchored her upswept hair, Charles turned her round and unzipped the back of her dress before sliding it off her shoulders. The dress and her hair fell together, leaving her naked except for her skimpy briefs.

She felt his hands tremble as they covered her breasts and she trembled herself at the warm, unfamiliar contact.

'Darling girl...don't let me rush you...it's not an ideal combination...a man who's starving and a virgin.'

She leaned back against him, feeling the pounding of his heart against her shoulderblade, the urgent desire charging his tall powerful body, and also the rigid control which was holding that fierce force in check, keeping his caresses gentle.

'Darling Charles...let me go a minute.'

Instantly she was released.

She was already barefoot and it took her two seconds to whip off her little silk briefs and toss them aside before starting to unbutton his shirt.

'But not a shy, shrinking virgin,' she said, as she tugged it out of his trousers and ran her hands over his chest. 'They died out a long time ago.'

She turned and bounced on to the bed, happy, confident, eager, holding out her arms to him.

Hours later, when the tide was on the turn and they had made love three times, they put on white towelling robes with the monogram *S F* on them, and went to the galley and made sandwiches which they took on deck with a bottle of Montrachet.

Sharing a lounger, with a table for their moonlight picnic alongside, they discussed and explained all that had puzzled them about each other's behaviour in the past before turning their minds to the future.

Snuggled in the crook of Charles's arm, Angel said, 'If we have a son I'd like, if you don't mind, to call him Ludovic.'

He gave her an affirmative squeeze. 'I wish I'd known your grandfather. Although I think you'd have been the way you are whoever had brought you up. I remember after your first appearance on TV, I brought you a newspaper cutting, and instead of snatching it from me to read what they'd said about you, you were more concerned about warming me up with mulled punch.' He gave her another hug. 'What a rotten Christmas that was! I wanted to fill a stocking for you...take you tobogganing somewhere...help you to decorate a tree. Instead of which I kicked my heels at a glitzy Long Island house party.'

'And I got the spinster's thimble in my slice of Carol's mother's Christmas pud, and cried over the inscription in the book you'd given me. Just *To Angel from Charles* and the year.'

She swung her feet to the deck and turned round to face him. 'Never mind, that's all in the past. Next Christmas, wherever we are, we'll fill stockings for each other. Not expensive books from Hatchards or solid gold trifles from Cartier paid for with plastic money. We'll go to the local market and find little *loving* presents. Oh, Charles, it's going to be so much fun from now on!'

He pulled her back into his arms, and presently Angel dozed with her head on his shoulder, waking to find the sun rising up from behind the horizon and the whole world the colour of roses.

Which, now that they were together, was the way it would always be.

DREAM SONG TITLES COMPETITION
HOW TO ENTER

Listed below are 5 incomplete song titles. To enter simply choose the missing word from the selection of words listed and write it on the dotted line provided to complete each song title.

A. . . . . DREAMS   LOVER

B. DAY DREAM . . . .   ELECTRIC

C. DREAM . . . .   CHRISTMAS

D. . . . . UPON A DREAM   BELIEVER

E. I'M DREAMING OF A WHITE . . . .   ONCE

When you have completed each of the song titles, fill in the box below, placing the songs in an order ranging from the one you think is the most romantic, through to the one you think is the least romantic.

Use the letter corresponding to the song titles when filling in the five boxes. For example: If you think C. is the most romantic song, place the letter C. in the 1st box.

	1st	2nd	3rd	4th	5th
LETTER OF CHOSEN SONG					

MRS/MISS/MR . . . .

ADDRESS. . . . .

. . . .

POSTCODE . . . . COUNTRY. . . . .

CLOSING DATE: 31st DECEMBER, 1990
PLEASE SEND YOUR COMPLETED ENTRY TO EITHER:
Dream Book Offer, Eton House, 18-24 Paradise Road, Richmond, Surrey, ENGLAND TW9 1SR.
OR (Readers in Southern Africa)
Dream Book Offer, IBS Pty Ltd., Private Bag X3010, Randburg 2125, SOUTH AFRICA.

✂ -

RULES AND CONDITIONS
Please retain this section.
FOR THE COMPETITION AND DREAM BOOK OFFER

1. These offers are open to all Mills & Boon readers with the exception of those living in countries where such a promotion is illegal, employees of the Harlequin Group of Companies, their agents, anyone directly connected with this offer and their families. **2.** All applications must be received by the closing date, 31st December, 1990. **3.** Responsibility cannot be accepted for entries lost, damaged or delayed in transit. Illegible applications will not be accepted. Proof of postage is not proof of receipt. **4.** The prize winner of the competition will be notified by post 28 days after the closing date. **5.** Only one application per household is permitted for the Competition and Dream Book. **6.** The prize for the competition will be awarded to the entrant who, in the opinion of the judges, has given the correct answers to the competition and in the event of a tie a further test of skill and judgement will be used to determine the winner. **7.** You may be mailed with other offers as a result of these applications.